NUTWOOD

John Harrold.

This book belongs to:

....

CONTENTS

STORIES BY **IAN ROBINSON**
ILLUSTRATED BY **JOHN HARROLD**
STORY COLOURING BY **GINA HART**

John Harrold.

RUPERT

THE EXPRESS ANNUAL

John Harrold.

Pedigree®

No 64

Published by Pedigree Books Limited
The Old Rectory, Matford Lane, Exeter, EX2 4PS

$18.95
RU64

RUPERT and

Three footballers set out to play
On Nutwood Common one fine day . . .

One winter morning Rupert and his pals decide to play football on Nutwood Common. "We'll take turns in goal," says Rupert. "You go first, Willie, while Podgy and I see how many we can score . . ." The little mouse is so quick on his feet that Rupert finds it impossible to beat him. "My turn!" calls Podgy and kicks the ball into the air. "Too high!" laughs Willie as it soars over his head. "Wait there, you two, I'll go and see where it's landed!"

the Forest Throne

When Podgy kicks the ball it clears
The makeshift goal – and disappears!

"I'll find it!" Willie calls. "You two
Aren't small enough to scramble through . . ."

Rupert and Podgy look on as Willie Mouse scrambles through a gap in the bushes. "The ball must be here somewhere!" he murmurs, then gives a sudden gasp. "What is it?" asks Rupert. "Is anything wrong?" "No!" calls Willie. "I've found something. It looks like a chair . . ." "Probably old junk," laughs Podgy. "No, it isn't broken," says Willie. "It's all shiny and new. I wish you could see it too! If the gap was bigger, you could squeeze through and join me . . ."

"I say!" he calls excitedly.
*"There's something I **wish** you could see!"*

RUPERT'S CHUMS ARE AMAZED

*The bushes part. "Look! Willie's there!
He's sitting in a golden chair!"*

*"I found it, hidden, out of view,
Somebody left it here, but who?"*

*"It granted your wish, like a spell,
I'll make one now, so we can tell . . ."*

*Stars fill the air and then a dish
Of sweets appears – it's Podgy's wish!*

As Willie speaks, the bushes quiver, then fly apart to show him seated on a wonderful golden chair. "What happened?" he blinks. "One moment, I was surrounded by leaves, then, suddenly, I could see you both . . ." "And we could see you!" marvels Rupert. "It looks like a throne!" gasps Podgy. "No wonder the owner hid it!" "If it was the owner!" says Willie. "Perhaps it's been stolen and left here by a gang of thieves?" "You might be right," nods Rupert. "We ought to fetch P.C. Growler . . ."

Just as the chums are about to go and tell Nutwood's policeman about their mysterious find, Podgy announces he has an idea . . . "What if this is a magic chair, one that grants wishes? When Willie wished we could see it, the bushes parted straightaway . . ." "Perhaps it does grant wishes," says Rupert. "But how can we tell?" "I'll make one!" says Podgy and sits in the gold chair. Almost at once, the air fills with stars and a dish of Turkish Delight appears. "Perfect!" beams Podgy.

RUPERT MAKES A WISH

The friends discuss what they should ask
The chair to do for its next task.

"I wish I knew . . ." says Rupert, then
The air fills with bright stars again.

The pals are all amazed to find
They're in a palace of some kind . . .

"Incredible!" blinks Willie Mouse.
"We must be in the owner's house!"

Hardly able to believe their luck, Rupert and Willie hop up into the chair to share Podgy's Turkish Delight. "It's delicious!" he laughs. "The best I've ever tasted." The three friends are so excited that all they can think of is what to wish for next. "An aeroplane!" says Willie. "We could fly over the whole of Nutwood." "Milkshakes!" beams Podgy. "I wish we could see where the chair came from!" murmurs Rupert. All at once, the air swirls with stars and Nutwood Common begins to fade . . .

To the chums' amazement, they suddenly find themselves in a strange building hung with curtains of colourful silk . . . "What happened?" blinks Willie. "Where are we?" "It looks like some sort of palace!" says Rupert. "I didn't mean to make a wish, but this must be mine. I wanted to see where the chair had come from." Climbing down cautiously, the three friends marvel at their magic adventure. "It's like a fairy tale!" whispers Willie. "Each wish is more wonderful than the last . . ."

RUPERT AND HIS PALS ARE CHASED

"It looks just like a storybook!
Let's go outside and take a look . . ."

"A fountain!" Podgy beams. "This wish
Is wonderful! I bet there's fish . . ."

Then, suddenly, an angry pair
Of Palace Guards appear. "Who's there?"

"This way!" calls Rupert. "Follow me!
Back to the chair, immediately!"

"Let's explore a bit, before we go back," says Podgy. "I'm not sure . . ." begins Rupert, but Willie agrees. "It would be a shame not to see any more," he declares. "We'll just peek at the courtyard, then go back to the chair." Outside, the chums find a beautiful fountain, surrounded by exotic trees and shrubs. "It's like a waterfall!" says Podgy. "I saw one in a picture once, with goldfish in the pool at the bottom." "Wait!" calls Rupert, but Podgy is determined to take a closer look . . .

Peering into the fountain, the pals see a cluster of shimmering, golden fish . . . "They look enormous!" says Podgy. "Who's there?" booms a voice. The pals spin round to see two guards advancing towards them. "Thieves!" growls one man. "Robbers!" nods the other. "They must have come to steal the Sultan's treasure . . ." "Quick!" calls Rupert. "Follow me! We've got to reach the golden chair before it's too late. If we make another wish we can escape back to Nutwood . . ."

RUPERT IS CAPTURED

The chums leap up and quickly tell
The chair to make another spell.

"It hasn't worked!" gasps Rupert. "No!"
The guards declare. "You shall not go!"

"Our Master, Zabac, knows the way
To deal with thieves! He'll make you pay!"

"Who are these strangers?" Zabac frowns.
"We found them in the palace grounds . . ."

With a sigh of relief, the three chums pile into the chair, just ahead of the angry guards. "Hold tight!" calls Rupert. "I'll tell it where to take us ..." Thinking hard, he chants a rhyme to command the magic chair. "Please help us in our hour of need. Return to Nutwood at top speed!" "It's not working!" gasps Podgy. "Surrender at once!" cry the palace guards. "The Sultan has given strict instructions to stop strangers entering the palace. Your attempts to flee are useless . . ."

"We're not thieves!" says Rupert as the guards lead the chums away. "We simply found ourselves in the palace and decided to look around . . ." "A likely tale!" scoffs one of the sentries. "Our Master, Zabac, will know how to deal with you. He guards his fortune jealously . . ." The pals are taken to a room hung with splendid silks, where a stern-looking figure sits on a pile of cushions. "What's this?" he demands. "Who are these strangers?" "Robbers, Excellency!" calls a guard.

"Thieves!" growls the Sultan angrily.
"You came to steal my gold from me!"

"No!" Podgy says. "It isn't true . . ."
"Enough!" cries Zabac. "Jail for you!"

"What now?" blinks Willie. "Who knows when
They'll ever let us go again?"

"The Sultan will decide! He deals
With thieves depending how he feels . . ."

"Kneel!" yells a guard as they approach the Sultan. "Zabac, the All-Powerful, will sit in judgment!" When he hears how the chums were found by the fountain, the Sultan frowns and tugs his beard. "We didn't come to steal anything," says Podgy but the guards call for silence. "It is enough that you were found in the courtyard!" booms Zabac. "Why else would you come but to steal my treasure? Take them away and lock them in the dungeons. I will decide what to do when we are sure that nothing is missing . . ."

No sooner has the Sultan spoken, than Rupert and his chums are marched off by the palace guard. "W . . . what do you think he'll do?" stammers Willie. "I don't know," says Rupert. "He doesn't seem very friendly!" "Halt!" orders a guard, while his companion unlocks a door. "This is where we'll keep you until His Excellency gives further orders." "How long?" asks Rupert. "Who knows?" shrugs the guard. "The Sultan is a busy man with many urgent matters to attend to . . ."

RUPERT HEARS A FRIENDLY VOICE

"Oh, dear!" sighs Rupert. "Now I see!
The chair grants one wish each – just three . . ."

A voice calls to the chums. "Hello!
I'm being held here too, you know . . ."

"My name is Salim. Zabac stole
My throne and took the Sultan's role!"

"I'll help you get away! Just do
Exactly what I tell you to . . ."

"This is terrible!" groans Podgy. "How will we ever get back to Nutwood?" "I don't know," admits Rupert. "The chair doesn't seem to work any more..." "Perhaps it only grants one wish each?" says Willie. "Of course!" sighs Podgy. "You used yours to show us the chair, I used mine to ask for Turkish Delight, while Rupert's wish is what brought us here in the first place . . ." "If only there was somebody here to help us," says Rupert. "Hello, there!" calls a voice. "I see that Zabac's caught you too!"

Hurrying to the window, Rupert sees a boy peering down from a nearby tower. "I'm a prisoner, too!" he calls. "My uncle locked me up when he declared himself Sultan!" "W . . . who are you?" blinks Rupert. "Salim," the boy replies. "It is *I* who should be Sultan, but Zabak has stolen my throne!" "So he's the thief!" cries Podgy. "And to think he called us robbers . . ." "Don't worry!" calls Salim. "I can help you escape, even though I'm held in this tower. Listen carefully and all will be well . . ."

RUPERT FINDS A TRAP DOOR

"The room you're in has a trap door –
It's under a chest on the floor . . ."

"Look!" Willie cries. "That must be where
The door is hidden – over there . . ."

The three chums drag the chest away.
"It's true! There's a way out! Hurray!"

"Wait!" Rupert calls. "We still can't get
The chair to take us back home yet . . ."

Salim explains that the chums have been locked in a storeroom nobody uses. "It has a secret passage built by my wise old grandfather," he whispers. "I found it by accident one day when I was exploring the palace. Look for an ornate chest, then pull it aside to reveal the hidden door . . ." "It must be that one!" says Willie, pointing excitedly. "Trust me!" calls Salim. "Zabac will never suspect until you're well away from the palace. His guards are so lazy, they won't even notice you've gone!"

Pulling at the heavy chest, Rupert and Podgy drag it clear to find a small trap-door hidden underneath. "Just as Salim said!" laughs Willie. The door opens to reveal a steep flight of steps but the pals all hesitate before clambering down. "What happens if we meet anyone?" says Willie. "And where do we go once we've managed to escape?" adds Podgy. "Nutwood must be miles away!" "You're right," nods Rupert. "Escaping from Zabac isn't enough. We need to find a way to get home . . ."

RUPERT LEADS THE WAY

"We need another wish! But how?
Of course! Back to the palace now . . ."

"Back?" Willie blinks. "But surely then
Zabac will lock us up again?"

"He might!" says Rupert. "But I plan
To make him help us, if I can . . ."

He peers out where the tunnel ends –
"The fountain!" Rupert tells his friends.

Rupert thinks hard for a moment, then suddenly smiles. "I know how we can get back to Nutwood!" he declares. "We'll use the golden chair . . ." "But we've spent all our wishes!" blinks Podgy. "And it means going back into the palace!" gasps Willie. "It's our only chance!" says Rupert. "If my plan works, we can even help Salim, too! Follow me closely and do exactly as I say . . ." Podgy and Willie clamber down as Rupert leads the way. "Quickly!" he calls. "There isn't a moment to lose!"

At the bottom of the stairs, the chums find a gloomy tunnel, which twists and turns underneath the palace. "I wonder where it comes out?" whispers Podgy. "We'll see soon," says Rupert. "That looks like the far end, with some more steps to climb . . ." Silently lifting the catch, Rupert pulls open the door and finds himself in broad daylight, with the sound of splashing water. "The courtyard!" he cries. "It couldn't be better. We're nearly back where we first arrived!"

RUPERT TRICKS THE GUARDS

"This way!" says Rupert. "Now we'll see
If my plan works! Just follow me . . ."

"Guards!" Willie gasps. "Let's run away!"
But Rupert tells his chums to stay.

He greets the sentries with a grin.
*"No locks and bars can keep **us** in!"*

"We're conjurers – let Zabac know –
Magicians, who can come and go!"

The courtyard seems deserted as Rupert leads the way back to the golden chair. "Follow me!" he calls. "It's important that we all keep together . . ." Turning a corner, the chums spot a pair of sentries blocking the way. "Quick!" cries Willie. "Let's make a run for it!" "Wait!" says Rupert. "If my plan works, they won't try to stop us, in fact, they'll help us escape . . ." "Help?" blinks Podgy. "Yes," whispers Rupert. "Just don't let them see you're afraid, and leave all the talking to me . . ."

To his pals' surprise, Rupert greets the guards and calmly asks for directions. "We're exploring the palace," he adds. "My friends grew tired of staying in the same room!" "How did you escape?" blinks a sentry. "I locked you up myself!" "We can come and go as we please!" laughs Rupert. "In Nutwood I am known as a great conjurer, who travels the world with his faithful assistants. Summon the Sultan and let him see! I will prove my power with a display of magic . . ."

*The Sultan scowls. "Can this be true?
What deeds of magic can you do?"*

*"My spells can make real gold appear!
I'll give a demonstration here!"*

*"How many gold coins would you like?
The weight of that boy seems just right . . ."*

*"My nephew, Salim, will enjoy
A magic trick. Quick! Fetch the boy!"*

The Sultan scowls as he approaches the chums. "What is the meaning of this? My soldiers tell me you escaped by magic . . ." "That's right!" says Rupert. "In my own land I am a famous conjurer, who can open all doors and fill empty coffers with heaps of gold . . ." "Gold?" asks the Sultan. "And jewels!" says Rupert. "My assistants and I can make them appear whenever we want. I'll show you, if you like . . ." "Yes!" nods the Sultan greedily. "A display of such magic would be most interesting!"

Convinced that Rupert is a real magician, the Sultan waits eagerly for the gold to appear. "I can produce a single coin, or a whole chest!" boasts Rupert. "Bring me the boy from that tower and I will give you his weight in gold!" Zabac looks up to where Rupert points, then orders the guards to bring Salim down. "Be quick about it!" he smiles. "My nephew will enjoy a conjuring trick. It's a shame he's not heavier, but even his weight should be a tidy sum!"

"Come on!" calls Zabac greedily.
"There's someone here for you to see . . ."

As Salim spots the chums he blinks,
But Rupert only smiles and winks.

"I need a chair to work the spell,
This way please – bring the boy as well . . ."

"That's perfect!" Rupert smiles. "Don't say
A word now till we're underway!"

"Come along!" calls Zabac. "There's no need to be afraid. I only want you to help this conjurer with one of his tricks . . ." Salim gasps as he catches sight of Rupert and fears his uncle has caught the chums trying to escape. To his surprise, Rupert gives a wink and pretends they have never met. "You're just the right size!" he declares. "Any heavier and the spell wouldn't work!" "Begin at once!" commands the Sultan. "If you can really conjure up gold, think how wealthy I will be . . ."

Telling the Sultan to be patient, Rupert announces that all he needs to start the spell is a chair. "I saw one as we explored the palace that will be perfect," he declares. "Follow me!" Rupert leads the way back to the golden chair which brought the chums from Nutwood. Salim smiles when he sees it, and is about to speak when Rupert cuts him short with a warning. "No one must interrupt the spell! Listen very carefully to my words and be sure to do exactly as I say . . ."

"*Sit still and wait for me to chant
The magic spell the chair will grant . . .*"

"*My two attendants need to stand
Next to the boy – on either hand . . .*"

"*The magic spell will work when you
Repeat my next words – say them too!*"

"*I wish to go to Nutwood! There!
Now, all climb on the magic chair!*"

Rupert tells Salim to climb up into the chair and sit still as a statue. "Don't worry!" he whispers. "I'll explain what I'm up to later . . ." As the Sultan looks on eagerly, Rupert declares that Podgy and Willie have a part to play too and tells them to stand on either side of the golden chair. When everything is ready, he starts to chant a spell . . . "Be patient now, it's nearly time. I'll summon up the gold in rhyme. I'll put my magic to the test and try to grant Zabac's request!"

"Is it working yet?" asks the Sultan, rubbing his hands at the thought of so much gold. "Soon!" declares Rupert. "But you mustn't interrupt the spell!" Turning to Salim, he starts to chant again. "To make what we desire appear, repeat the next words that you hear. The special phrase you need to know is 'Nutwood's where we wish to go!'" Bounding forward, he jumps up on to the chair and tells his chums to climb up too. "Make the same wish!" he tells Salim. "Say it out loud . . ."

19

RUPERT'S TRICK WORKS

"A trick!" blinks Zabac. "Come back here!"
Too late – the pals all disappear . . .

"We're home!" cries Podgy. "Now I see!
What Salim wished was bound to be . . ."

"You're safe now, Salim! Zabac's far
Away. He won't know where you are!"

"The Sultan!" Willie gasps. "What now?
He must have followed us somehow . . ."

Salim blinks, then says the words, "I wish to go to Nutwood . . ." All at once, the Sultan and his men start to fade away and the chums are surrounded by a haze of shining stars. "It's working!" calls Podgy as he hangs on tight. "You really are a magician!" "No!" smiles Rupert as the stars clear and they find themselves safely back on Nutwood Common. "It's the chair that worked the magic. It granted Salim's wish, just as it granted each of ours . . ." "What now?" gasps the startled boy.

"Don't be frightened!" smiles Rupert. "You'll be safe here." "What about Zabac?" asks Salim. "He'll be furious when he realises how you tricked him. If he finds out where we've gone, he might try to come to Nutwood too . . ." "Not without the golden chair!" says Rupert. "Don't forget we brought that with us too!" Salim nods, and agrees that his fears are groundless. Just then, the pals hear voices nearby and see two shadowy figures approaching. "The Sultan!" wails Willie. "He's followed us after all!"

RUPERT MEETS A MAGICIAN

"It's Hitash!" Salim cheers. "Hurray!
He's on our side! Don't run away . . ."

*"He's a Magician! It's **his** chair –*
He travels in it everywhere . . ."

"You say that Zabac seized the throne?
It's all my fault! I should have known!"

"I'll make a spell to set things right –
And give your uncle quite a fright!"

As the chums turn to flee, Salim calls, "Wait! It's Hitash. *He's* not one of the Sultan's men . . ." Turning back, Rupert sees an elderly man walking across the common together with the Wise Old Goat. "Salim!" blinks the stranger. "However did you get here?" "In your golden chair," smiles the boy and tells how Rupert and his friends arrived at the palace and rescued him from Zabac. "Hitash is our Court Magician," he explains. "A mighty wizard who travels far and wide in search of herbs and berries . . ."

Hitash explains that he came to Nutwood to ask the Wise Old Goat about a rare moss. When he hears of Zabac's threats, he shakes his head and frowns. "I should never have trusted him," he declares. "The time has come to set things straight! *You* are the rightful heir to the throne, Salim. Zabac will be Sultan no longer!" As Rupert looks on, the old man produces a wand from his bag and chants a magic spell. The air fills with stars and a crystal ball appears, glowing with dazzling light . . .

"Zabac! We thought you were a friend!
Your crooked rein is at an end . . ."

"Salim is Sultan! You can stay
Locked up for now – out of the way!"

Salim thanks all the chums and then
Returns to the palace again.

"Bravo!" the Wise Goat smiles. "Well done!
*I **wish** I could have seen the fun . . ."*

To Rupert's astonishment, the crystal ball shimmers, then clears to reveal Zabac, quailing before the magician's unblinking gaze. "Your reign is over!" Hitash declares. "Salim has told me of your treachery and how you imprisoned the visitors from Nutwood." "No!" pleads the Sultan. "They tricked me with a promise of gold. I would have let them go . . . eventually!" "Enough!" says Hitash. "It's *your* turn to be imprisoned now. Salim is the new Sultan! Long may he prosper . . ."

Now that the palace is safe, Salim tells the chums he must return at once. "Thank you for all your help!" he smiles. "Perhaps I may return and see more of Nutwood?" "Of course!" calls Rupert as the golden chair fades from sight. "What an adventure!" laughs Podgy. "Rupert made a marvellous conjurer!" "Really?" says the Wise Old Goat. "I wish I could have seen him!" "No more wishes today!" calls Rupert. "I think we've had our share!"

RUPERT
and the Gold-Rush

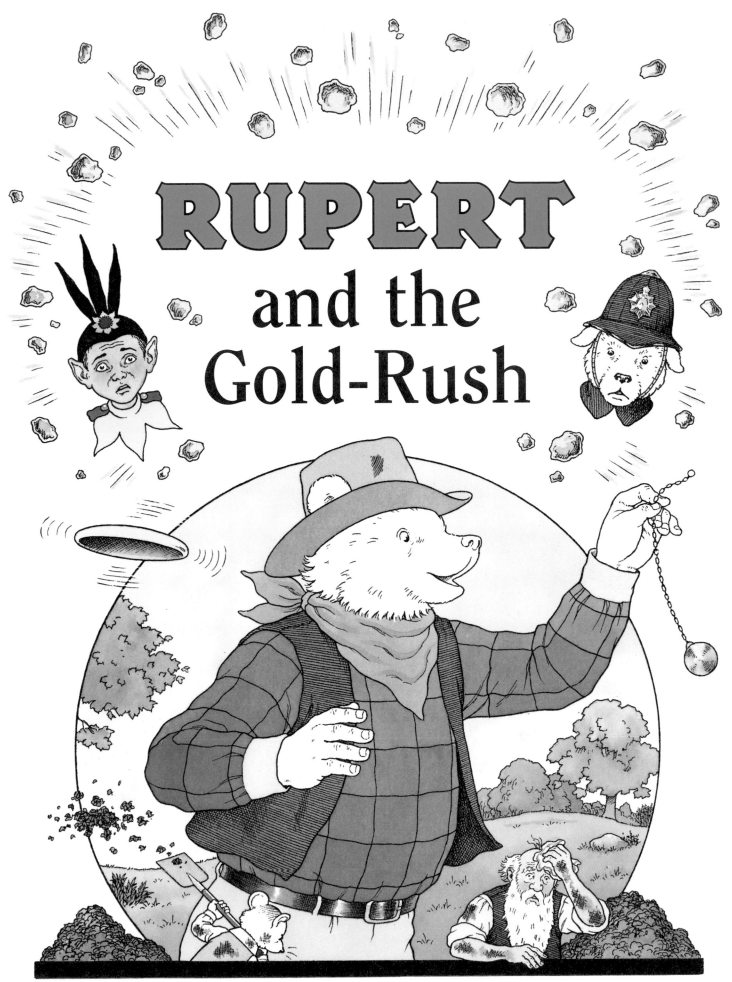

John Harrold.

RUPERT HAS A LETTER

It's summer and the Nutwood chums
Are playing, when the postman comes . . .

"This letter's come from far away –
Montana, in the U.S.A."

The chums run in to Mrs. Bear –
"A letter for you!" call the pair.

"It's Uncle Grizzly! Let me see . . .
He's on his way here, gracious me!"

It is the middle of the summer holidays and Rupert and Bill are playing at cowboys in the garden . . . "Nobody beats the Quickdraw Kid!" warns Bill. "We'll see about that!" laughs Rupert. "I think your pistol's nearly run out of water!" Just then, the postman arrives with a special delivery. "It's an airmail letter from America!" he explains. "The postmark says Montana . . ." Rupert looks at the letter excitedly. "I wonder who it's from?" he says. "I'll take it in to my parents straightaway!"

Rupert and Bill hurry indoors with the unexpected letter. "It's from America!" calls Rupert. "I can't wait to see who's sent it . . ." "Uncle Grizzly!" smiles his mother. "He's planning a trip to England and wants to come and see us, here in Nutwood." "That will be fun!" says Mr. Bear. "When does he say he might be coming?" "Tuesday, the 28th," blinks Rupert's mother. "But that's tomorrow! His letter must have been held up in the post. We'd better get everything ready!"

RUPERT'S UNCLE GRIZZLY ARRIVES

Next morning, Rupert hears a sound.
A taxi stops, then turns around . . .

"It's Grizzly!" Rupert gives a cheer.
"Well, howdy folks! At last, I'm here!"

"Say, little Nephew, Just for fun –
I've brought a gift for everyone . . ."

"A frisbee!" Rupert gasps. "Bravo!
Let's take it out and have a go . . ."

Next morning, Rupert and his parents have just finished tidying the house when they hear a car drawing up outside . . . "It's a taxi!" calls Rupert. "Uncle Grizzly must be here!" Hurrying up the garden path, he finds his uncle standing at the gate. "Howdy, nephew!" smiles Grizzly. "I sure am glad to have arrived in Nutwood. Feels as if I've been in the saddle for days!" "Grizzly!" calls Mrs. Bear. "How lovely to see you again! Come in and tell us all about your journey . . ."

Rupert is thrilled to meet his American uncle. "Are you really a cowboy?" he asks. "From cowboy country!" laughs Grizzly. "Though *I* live up high in the mountains . . ." Opening his bag, he produces a hat for Mr. Bear and a jar of maple syrup for Rupert's mother. "This is for you," he tells Rupert. "All the youngsters back home play frisbee, so I thought you might enjoy it too . . ." "Thank you!" says Rupert. "We can play together, up on Nutwood Common." "Sounds great!" smiles Grizzly.

"The weather's so fine I thought you
Might like to have a picnic too . . ."

"So, this is Nutwood!" Grizzly smiles.
*"Where **I** live mountains stretch for miles . . ."*

In Nutwood, everybody stares
To see a cowboy with the Bears . . .

"We'll picnic by the river, then
Walk back down the High Street again . . ."

"It's such a nice day, I thought we'd go for a picnic!" says Mrs. Bear. "Swell!" says Grizzly. "I've heard so much about Nutwood, I can hardly wait to have a proper look round . . ." As the Bears set off towards the village, Uncle Grizzly tells Rupert how different everything is to the Rockies, where he lives. "All these thatched houses!" he laughs. "It's just how I imagined. So peaceful too! You folk sure are lucky to live in such a pretty spot . . ."

As the Bears make their way through Nutwood they meet P.C. Growler, who is amazed to see a grown-up in cowboy clothes . . . "Howdy!" smiles Grizzly. "You must be the local sheriff. My nephew here is taking me on a tour of the village." "Pleased to meet you!" blinks the policeman. "I hope you enjoy your visit to England." "This way!" says Mrs. Bear. "I thought we'd have our picnic by the river." "Great idea!" beams Rupert's uncle. "Then maybe we'll do more sightseeing later . . ."

RUPERT THROWS THE FRISBEE

Before the picnic, Grizzly shows
His nephew some good frisbee throws . . .

"Well caught!" he calls. "And now we'll see
If you can throw it back to me!"

"Here goes!" cries Grizzly. "I'll catch that!"
Success! But now he's lost his hat . . .

"Don't worry, Rupert, luckily
This river flows quite sluggishly."

While Rupert's parents find a grassy spot by the riverbank and start to unpack the picnic, Uncle Grizzly agrees to play frisbee with his nephew. "It's easy, once you get the hang of it!" he smiles. "We'll start off with some short throws, then move further apart." Rupert watches carefully as his uncle throws the brightly coloured disc towards him. "Well done!" calls Grizzly as he jumps up and catches it. "Now it's your turn to toss it back to me. Aim high and let it fall . . ."

Following his uncle's advice, Rupert pitches the frisbee up into the air . . . "Good throw!" calls Grizzly, leaping up to catch it. As he jumps, his hat flies off and tumbles into the nearby stream. "Oh, dear!" says Rupert. "It's wet through . . ." "Never mind!" smiles the visitor. "A drop of water never hurt a hat. I'm sure we'll be able to get it back. It's lucky the river isn't faster, though. A mountain stream would carry your hat off before you even noticed it was gone!"

RUPERT DISCOVERS GOLD

"I'll get it!" Rupert cries. "Not far
To reach now . . . Bravo! There you are . . ."

"Well done!" smiles Grizzly. "That's how you
Can go prospecting for gold too!"

As Rupert swirls the hat he blinks –
"I really have found gold!" he thinks . . .

"Gold!" Grizzly gasps. "I'd no idea
That folk could go prospecting here!"

Reaching out for his uncle's hat, Rupert manages to catch hold of the brim just in time to stop it sinking . . . "Bravo!" cheers Grizzly. "You've saved me from getting my boots wet!" As Rupert hands back the hat, he sees it is still full of water. "Reminds me of my prospecting days!" laughs Grizzly. "When you're out on the trail you can use your hat to pan for gold . . ." "Gold?" blinks Rupert. "Sure!" nods his uncle. "You just wait for the water to drain away, then see if there's anything there . . ."

Rupert is fascinated by his uncle's talk of prospecting . . . "You just swirl the hat round gently, then see what's there." "Gold!" gasps Rupert. "That's right!" nods Grizzly. "What every prospector dreams of finding . . ." "No, there's gold *here!*" cries Rupert, handing his uncle the hat. "I can see it glinting at the bottom!" Grizzly peers at the hat in astonishment, then carefully picks out a gleaming nugget. "It sure looks like gold!" he blinks. "I didn't know you had any in England!"

RUPERT TELLS THE PROFESSOR

"It **looks** like gold," says Mr. Bear.
"But English finds are very rare . . ."

"The Old Professor! He'll know what
To do to test the gold we've got."

"Hello, Professor! Come with me,
There's something that you've got to see . . ."

"It **could** be gold! It's very bright . . .
I'll test it to see if you're right!"

Mr. Bear is astonished by Rupert's find as well ... "I suppose it *could* be gold!" he shrugs. "They sometimes find it in streams, though I've never heard of any from Nutwood . . ." "Back home, we'd have it assayed next, then stake a claim . . ." says Grizzly. "Assayed?" blinks Rupert. "Tested," explains his uncle. "There are other metals that look like gold, but they're worthless. Only a test can tell us what we've got." "The Professor . . ." murmurs Rupert. "I wonder if he might know?"

The Professor and his servant, Bodkin, have been out by the river looking for butterflies. When he hears about Rupert's discovery, he hurries over to look at the golden nuggets. "How extraordinary!" he gasps. "It certainly looks like gold . . ." "Just what *I* said!" nods Uncle Grizzly. "But what if it's only Pyrites?" "Fool's Gold?" blinks the Professor. "It might be, I suppose. If I tested a nugget in my laboratory, I'd soon be able to tell. We can go there straightaway, if you'd like . . ."

"We've never found gold here before,
But once we've tested we'll be sure . . ."

"One piece will show us what this is –
Real gold's so pure it shouldn't fizz . . ."

"Yee-ha!" whoops Grizzly in delight.
"It's gold! Look, Rupert! You were right!"

"Thanks, Prof! Now we know that it's gold,
The Sheriff's Office should be told . . ."

"It's rather exciting to find gold in Nutwood!" says the Professor as he leads Rupert and Grizzly across the fields to his tower. "I think there was once a coal mine near Popton, but that was hundreds of years ago. I don't remember *anything* quite like this . . ." When they reach his laboratory, the Professor fills a jar with liquid and tips out the nuggets to choose a good sample. "Watch carefully," he says. "Most metals will dissolve immediately. Real gold is different. It stays just as it is . . ."

Everyone looks on nervously as the Professor drops the nugget into the beaker . . . "Conclusive proof!" he smiles. "There's no doubt that this is real gold!" "Yee-ha!" whoops Grizzly. "We've hit paydirt, little Nephew! Who knows *how* much more there might be out there?" "Hard to tell . . ." murmurs the Professor. "You'd need to pan the river for quite a while before you'd be sure." "Plenty of time for that later!" declares Rupert's uncle. "First we've got to stake our claim . . ."

RUPERT STAKES HIS CLAIM

*"We've got to take our gold to show
The local sheriff, let him know . . ."*

*"Gold!" Growler blinks. "A claim? Oh, dear!
Perhaps I'd better keep it here . . ."*

*"The best thing for this gold would be
To log it as Lost Property . . ."*

*"Hello!" says Mr. Bear. "We guessed
Your nugget must have passed the test . . ."*

Uncle Grizzly tells Rupert that when a prospector finds gold, he needs to stake his claim before anyone else can beat him to it . . . "Sheriff's Office is the normal place!" he says. "I guess that means Constable Growler . . ." Rupert leads his uncle to Nutwood's police station, where the pair proudly display their gleaming find. "Gold!" blinks Growler. "I don't think that's mentioned in Regulations!" "You could put it in your strong-room," suggests Grizzly. "The main thing's to register our claim . . ."

P.C. Growler thinks hard for a moment, then decides to enter Rupert's gold in his "Lost Property" ledger . . . "I know it wasn't really lost," he shrugs, "but at least this will show who found it!" "Good!" nods Grizzly, "Now I guess we ought to go back to join the picnic . . ." "Sorry we've taken so long!" says Rupert when the pair arrive. "Not to worry!" smiles Mr. Bear. "It's an interesting find. I've never heard of Nutwood gold before. Perhaps they'll put it on display in Nutchester museum . . ."

RUPERT'S FATHER READS THE NEWS

Next morning, Mr. Bear reads how
The Nutwood gold is big news now!

"Oh, no!" groans Grizzly. "Now you'll see
How crazy a gold-rush can be!"

"A gold-rush?" Mr. Bear feels sure
That nothing like that lies in store . . .

At first it seems that he is right –
Then Rupert's pals come into sight!

Next morning, as everyone is having breakfast, Rupert's father hears the paper arrive and brings it in to show the others . . . "I say!" he gasps. "Look at the front page! It's all about Rupert's discovery ..." "Oh, no!" groans Grizzly. "I was worried something like this might happen. It will be the Klondike all over again! People will come from far and wide, folk will start digging all along the river and your quiet little village will never know a moment's peace!"

"Surely there won't be a gold-rush in Nutwood?" says Mr. Bear. "It happened in America, but that was long ago and, besides, things are different here . . ." "We'll see!" shrugs Grizzly. "I reckon gold's the same the whole world over." The Bears decide to go back to the river to see if anything has changed. "It seems peaceful enough, so far," smiles Mr. Bear. Just then, Rupert spots two of his chums, coming across the common. "Bingo and Podgy," he blinks. "They're carrying a sieve!"

RUPERT SEES THE GOLD-RUSH

*"Hello!" says Bingo. "Everyone
Has gone prospecting. Join the fun!"*

*"My new machine will tell us where
To dig. It shows if metal's there . . ."*

*More prospectors come into view –
They're heading for the river too!*

*"Gold-fever!" Grizzly gasps. "Look, all
Of Nutwood's been caught in its thrall!"*

"Hello!" says Bingo. "Are you on your way to the river?" "Yes," blinks Rupert. "But how did you know?" "Everyone's going!" says Podgy. "They're all hoping to strike gold . . ." "That's why I've brought my metal detector," explains Bingo. "It lights up if there's anything there. Takes the guesswork out of prospecting!" "Smart thinking!" nods Grizzly. "Reckon you're in with a chance, if the others haven't got there first . . ." "Good luck!" mutters Mr. Bear. "I'll see you all at lunch time . . ."

As Rupert and his uncle get nearer to the river, they see that Podgy wasn't exaggerating . . . "Everyone in Nutwood must be here!" gasps Rupert. "Gold-fever!" sighs Grizzly. "It's the same the whole world over . . ." "Hello, Rupert!" calls Reggie Rabbit. "You'll need a net, if you've come to look for gold. Nobody's found any yet, although I'm sure it's only a matter of time!" "I guess he's right!" murmurs Grizzly. "That will really open the floodgates! Nutwood will be completely overrun!"

RUPERT'S UNCLE IS WORRIED

As Bingo searches, the chums hear
A heavy lorry drawing near . . .

"Good morning, folks! I hear you've got
Gold hidden in this charming spot!"

"It's just as well that nobody
Has found gold yet, just you and me!"

Next moment, Rupert hears a cry . . .
An Elf is calling him, but why?

With new arrivals still joining the throng of hopeful prospectors, Rupert and Grizzly stand staring in amazement at what their find has started . . . "Keep watching the light," Bingo tells Podgy. "As soon as it glows, we'll know where to dig." Before long, the Nutwood crowd is joined by an outsider, from a large mining company. "Morning, folks!" he smiles. "We heard the news and decided to see if it was true. Valuable commodity, gold. Not something you find every day!"

"Does anyone know the spot where gold was found?" asks the mining man. "No," admits Reggie. "No-one seems certain, but it must be *somewhere* along here . . ." "Not a word!" whispers Grizzly. "It's our secret Rupert. Let's keep it that way!" The pair are about to leave when Rupert suddenly hears somebody calling his name . . . "An Autumn Elf!" he gasps. "I wonder what he wants? It must be important to risk being seen by such a crowd. Luckily, they're all too busy to notice . . ."

RUPERT VISITS THE ELVES' H.Q.

"What's happening? Have they found gold?
If it's true our Chief should be told . . ."

"Come on! There's no time for delay –
I'll take you to him straightaway . . ."

The Elf leads Grizzly underground.
"Amazing!" he blinks, looking round . . .

"This way!" the Elf says. "It's not far –
I'll show you where Headquarters are . . ."

"Rupert!" says the Elf. "What's happened? Has the whole of Nutwood gone mad?" When he hears about the gold-rush, the Elf shakes his head and frowns. "I *thought* that's what they were up to, but it seemed too strange to be true . . ." "There is gold here, though!" says Rupert. "Uncle Grizzly and I found some nuggets yesterday." "Of course there's gold!" says the Elf. "There's always been gold under Nutwood, but nobody knew, except us and the Imps of Spring! You'd better come and see the Chief . . ."

The Elf leads Rupert and his uncle down through a hidden trapdoor to a rocky tunnel. "Amazing!" blinks Grizzly. "How far does it go?" "All the way to Headquarters!" replies the Elf. "It's a bit of a tight fit though, you'll have to mind your head . . ." "Must have taken years to dig this out!" says Grizzly as they make their way along the winding passage. "No wonder you know all about Nutwood's gold . . ." "This is only the beginning!" laughs the Elf. "The tunnels go on for miles and miles . . ."

RUPERT HEARS WHAT IS WRONG

"These visitors can tell you more
About the great big crowd we saw . . ."

The Chief Elf looks grim when he's told
How everyone's searching for gold.

"We can't have mining here, you know!
Just look at where our tunnels go . . ."

"Too late!" says Grizzly. "I can hear
The sound of digging somewhere near!"

The Elf leads Rupert and his uncle into a large room full of dials, switches and flashing lights . . . "Visitors, sir!" he announces. "They can tell you more about what's happening by the river . . ." "I'm glad that someone can!" says the Chief. "The whole of Nutwood seems to be splashing about up there!" "They're looking for gold!" explains Rupert. "I found some nuggets yesterday, and now everyone in the village has decided to try their luck . . ." "Prospecting!" gasps the Chief. "This is terrible!"

Rupert wonders why the Chief Elf is so upset by people panning for gold . . . "It's not the gold!" he explains. "It's when they start digging that things will get serious . . ." Pointing to a map on the wall, he shows the visitors how the whole of Nutwood is riddled with tunnels, leading away from the village and off across the fields. "They're vital for our work!" he says. "We need them to travel underground without being seen." "Listen!" says Grizzly. "I can hear something! Sounds like a pick-axe . . ."

RUPERT'S UNCLE HAS A PLAN

*"We'll go back up above ground now
And stop the prospectors, somehow . . ."*

*"It's my fault, Rupert! Let's look round
And see what everyone has found . . ."*

*To their dismay, the worried pair
See people digging everywhere . . .*

*Then Grizzly smiles. "I have a plan
To stop them all. I'm sure we can . . ."*

"We'd better get back above ground!" Grizzly tells the Chief Elf. "From the sound of things, there isn't a moment to lose . . ." Rupert and his uncle emerge from the secret entrance and make their way back towards the river. "How are we going to stop people from digging?" asks Rupert. "They're all convinced they'll find gold . . ." "I don't know yet!" says Grizzly. "But there must be *something* we can do. It's my fault all this started, Rupert. I don't want Nutwood's gold-rush to end in disaster . . ."

Back on Nutwood Common, the prospectors are still busy searching for gold . . . "This is even worse than I'd thought!" says Grizzly. "Everybody has started digging. It won't be long before someone falls into an Elves' tunnel! We've got to stop them, Rupert, before it's too late . . ." The pair think hard for a moment, then Rupert's uncle gives a sudden chuckle. "Might just do the trick!" he murmurs. "What?" blinks Rupert. "A bit of subterfuge . . ." smiles Grizzly. "Come on, Nephew! Follow me!"

"We'll need the Professor's help too!
Let's tell him what we plan to do . . ."

A little later, Grizzly comes
To try prospecting with the chums . . .

"Before you dig, you need to try
To find out where the gold will lie . . ."

"A pendulum will show you where . . .
It's still – that means there's nothing there!"

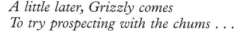

To Rupert's surprise, Uncle Grizzly leads the way across Nutwood Common towards the Professor's tower . . . "Should have thought of this sooner!" he laughs. "There's only one way to stop a gold-rush – and that's to fight fire with fire . . ." A little while later, Rupert and his uncle appear on the common carrying spades and a pick-axe. "Come to join the search?" asks Willie Mouse. "That's right!" nods Grizzly. "Reckon it's time for a bit of American know-how!"

As Grizzly appears, everyone stops digging and gathers round to see what he is up to . . . "The first thing you've got to do is find out where to dig!" declares Rupert's uncle. "Real prospectors can track gold down, like some folk do for water . . ." Taking a watch from his waistcoat pocket, he holds it out at arm's length and walks slowly towards the river. "Nothing yet!" he declares. "You'll see it move when we come to gold. That will be the spot to dig. Just mark my words . . ."

RUPERT'S UNCLE JOINS THE DIG

Then Grizzly's watch begins to swing . . .
"Eureka! Now we've found something!"

He digs a big hole in the ground –
"This spot is where gold's to be found!"

The hole gets deeper. "Nothing yet!"
Then Grizzly winks. "It's time! Get set . . ."

He shakes his sleeve and suddenly
Calls out, "Rupert! What's this I see?"

For a long time nothing seems to happen. Grizzly walks solemnly across Nutwood Common, with everybody staring at his watch. Suddenly, it starts to sway . . . "Eureka!" he calls. "The rest will be easy. All we've got to do now is dig . . ." Rupert helps his uncle to dig a deep hole. "Keep going!" smiles Grizzly. "It will be a while before we strike gold. Normally it's quite a way down. Don't be put off, though. I'm *certain* we'll find what we're looking for . . ."

Rupert and his uncle keep digging until they have made a deep pit. "Are you sure you've got the right spot?" calls Bingo. "My detector didn't show any metal down there . . ." "Sure I'm sure!" laughs Grizzly. "In fact, I'd say we're due to strike lucky any moment now!" Turning to Rupert, he winks secretly and shakes his sleeve. Unseen by the onlookers, a golden nugget tumbles to the bottom of the hole, glinting and gleaming as it falls. "Bless me!" calls Grizzly. "What have we here?"

RUPERT SEES ANOTHER FIND

"Gold!" Grizzly cries. "Just look at what
*We've found! I **knew** this was the spot . . ."*

The prospectors all stand and stare –
"Just think of all the gold that's there!"

"Hello!" the Old Professor cries.
"You've found more gold! What a surprise . . ."

"I've come to test the finds, you see,
To check them, scientifically . . ."

"Gold!" declares Grizzly, holding the gleaming nugget up for everyone to see . . . "I *knew* we'd find it here if we kept on digging. Can't beat a pendulum, you see! My old grandfather taught me that. A trick he learnt back in California . . ." "Amazing!" blinks Gaffer Jarge as he peers at Grizzly's find. "To think of gold being under Nutwood Common for all these years!" "That man from the mining company should see this!" says Freddy Fox. "It must be worth a fortune!"

Everybody is so busy marvelling at the gold nugget that they hardly notice the Professor and Bodkin strolling across the common towards the excited circle . . . "Hello!" says the inventor. "Is that a piece of gold I see? What luck! Bodkin and I were just on our way to test the latest finds . . ." "Test?" asks Grizzly. "Why, yes!" nods the Professor. "Scientific proof that Nutwood's gold is top grade. I've brought all the chemicals with me. A simple experiment is all it will take . . ."

RUPERT'S UNCLE IS DISAPPOINTED

The liquid starts to fizz – "Oh, dear!
This isn't gold at all, I fear!"

The mining man is most dismayed –
"It's fool's gold! Worthless, I'm afraid!"

"Shucks!" Grizzly sighs. "Just goes to show,
Where gold's concerned, you never know . . ."

The last prospectors leave and then
The mining man drives off again . . .

The crowd look on expectantly as the Professor drops Grizzly's gold into a beaker of liquid . . . To their amazement it starts to fizz and bubble, while the nugget dissolves like a lump of sugar! "Oh, dear," sighs the Professor. "What a shame! This isn't gold at all. It's only pyrites . . ." "Fool's gold?" blinks the man from the mining company. "That's no use to me! Looks like gold, of course, but it's completely worthless! Just as well you came along, Professor . . ."

"Shucks!" says Uncle Grizzly. "I felt *sure* we'd struck lucky! Guess even the old pendulum gets it wrong sometimes . . ." As news of his mistake travels, Nutwood's dejected prospectors abandon their search and return to the village. Rupert and his uncle stay behind to fill in the big hole they have dug. "Never mind!" says Grizzly as they watch the man from the mining company drive off in his lorry. "At least we had some fun. Perhaps Nutwood will be better off without a gold mine, after all!"

RUPERT RECOVERS HIS GOLD

"Well done, Professor!" Grizzly beams.
"The gold rush has stopped now, it seems!"

"There's one last thing for us to do –
That's put an end to our claim too . . ."

The pair return to claim their find –
*"We'd better not leave **this** behind . . ."*

"A shame we won't be millionaires,
But it was fun!" Growler declares.

"Well done, Professor!" laughs Grizzly. "You sure fooled everyone with that nugget of yours! Fool's gold is the right name for it. Now they'll never disturb the river bank!" "Quite right!" nods the Professor. "Whatever's down there can stay where it is, as far as I'm concerned. Peace and quiet are Nutwood's *real* treasures . . ." A little later, Rupert and his uncle return to the police station to visit P.C. Growler. "Hello!" he says. "Sorry to hear your bad news!"

"It's hard to believe this isn't real gold!" says P.C. Growler as he takes Rupert's find from the safe. "Yes," sighs Grizzly. "It sure looks like the real McCoy . . ." Wrapping the nuggets up carefully, he puts them in his pocket, while the policeman writes, "Returned to owner" in his Lost Property ledger. "That's that, I suppose!" shrugs Growler as he bids the pair farewell. "Pity we aren't all going to be millionaires but at least everyone enjoyed the fun!"

RUPERT SEES THE DIG ABANDONED

"The paper says we got it wrong –
Just worthless fool's gold all along!"

"Let's hope the diggers all agree!
We'll soon see, Rupert. Come with me . . ."

"Look!" Rupert blinks. "You'd never guess –
Somebody's cleared up all the mess!"

They hear a call – an Elf appears.
"The diggers have all gone!" he cheers.

Next morning, Rupert's father shows how the newspaper has brought an end to Nutwood's gold-rush . . . "Fool's gold!" he gasps. "I suppose it just goes to show how things aren't always what they seem . . ." "You're right there!" nods Grizzly. "But at least Nutwood should soon be back to peace and quiet!" Before he leaves, Grizzly decides to stroll down to the river and take one last look at the scene of all the excitement . . . "Let's hope our plan's done the trick!" he tells Rupert.

When Rupert and his uncle arrive at the river they are surprised to find that everything is already back to normal . . . "No sign of the diggings!" gasps Grizzly. "It's as if the whole thing was a dream." "A nightmare, you mean!" laughs an Elf, emerging from behind a clump of bushes. "We've been putting things straight ever since the last prospectors left. The Chief didn't want any clues, in case that mining man came back." "No danger of that!" laughs Grizzly. "I'm sure you've seen the last of him!"

RUPERT'S UNCLE SAYS GOODBYE

"I don't know what you had to do,
But our home's safe now – thanks to you!"

"You're welcome!" Grizzly smiles. "I'm sure
You won't be troubled any more . . ."

"Goodbye!" smiles Grizzly. "Hope to see
You next year, when you visit me . . ."

"A silver dollar!" Rupert blinks.
"It shines like Nutwood's gold," he thinks.

"I don't know how you made everybody leave, but you certainly kept your promise!" declares the Elf. "Let's just say it's a secret!" smiles Grizzly. "I don't think anyone in Nutwood will be digging for gold here again . . ." "Good!" says the Elf. "Then I can tell the Chief the tunnels are out of danger." "Safe as houses!" nods Grizzly. "And now I'd better be on my way. Got a long journey ahead of me, Nephew. Back to the Rockies and my home in the hills . . ."

"It sure has been fun, visiting Nutwood!" smiles Grizzly as he says goodbye to Mr. and Mrs. Bear. "Though I never thought I'd see an English gold-rush . . ." Before he leaves, he takes a gleaming coin from his pocket and hands it to Rupert. "A silver dollar!" he chuckles. "Next best thing to striking gold. Come and see me in America, little Nephew and we'll try our hand at prospecting again . . ."

RUPERT
and the
Skylark

John Harrold.

RUPERT FINDS A STRANGE SHOE

*"Hurrah!" smiles Rupert. "Spring is here.
The Winter's over, till next year!"*

*"A bird!" he thinks. "I wonder why
It's landed? It's too tired to fly!"*

*"It's not a bird at all!" he thinks.
"It's someone's sandal!" Rupert blinks.*

*"But where's it from?" He tries to guess.
"It's Ottoline's – her fancy dress!"*

It is a sunny Spring morning in Nutwood and Rupert has decided to go for a walk across the common . . . "Thank goodness Winter is finally over!" he smiles. "I was beginning to think it would never end!" Everywhere Rupert looks he sees flowers blooming, trees coming into leaf and birds returning from their Winter migration. All of a sudden, he spots a strange bird lying in a clump of long grass. "I hope it's all right!" he blinks. "Perhaps it's exhausted after flying so far . . ."

Trying not to startle the bird, Rupert tip-toes forward to take a closer look . . . "I don't believe it!" he laughs. "It isn't a bird at all! Somebody's lost a sandal. It's like an ordinary shoe, but with wings!" As he looks at the sandal, Rupert wonders where it can have come from. "It must be part of somebody's fancy dress costume!" he smiles. "Ottoline, I expect! She's always dressing up in old-fashioned clothes. I suppose she dropped it on her way across the common . . ."

RUPERT MAKES A DISCOVERY

Before he goes on, Rupert tries
The sandal that he's found for size . . .

He feels a tingle in his toes –
"It's from the sandal, I suppose!"

With every step that Rupert takes
He marvels at the leaps he makes . . .

"The sandal's feathers must be why
I'm able to jump up so high."

As Rupert looks more closely at the sandal, it seems too big to belong to Ottoline. "It fits over the top of my shoe!" he blinks. "I wonder what it's like to wear?" Buckling the sandal, he feels his foot start to tingle, almost as though he is being tickled… "How odd!" he murmurs. "I wonder if it's something to do with the feathers?" When Rupert tries walking he gets another surprise . . . "It's springy!" he gasps. "I can bounce up and down like a pogo-stick!"

With the winged sandal on his foot, Rupert finds he can jump higher and higher . . . "This is fun!" he laughs. "I feel as though I could hop all the way across the common . . ." Before long, he reaches a little stream. Although it would normally be too wide to cross, he takes a flying jump and clears it in a single bound! As Rupert's balance improves, he finds he can jump even higher, leaping over rocks and bushes without any trouble at all. "I feel as if I could fly!" he marvels.

RUPERT MEETS A STRANGER

The running jump that Rupert tries
Is so enormous that he flies!

To his astonishment he sees
A stranger, high above the trees . . .

"Hello, there!" Rupert gives a yell –
"I'm up above the trees as well!"

The boy has a winged sandal too –
"What luck!" he laughs. "You've found my shoe!"

As soon as Rupert starts to *think* about flying, he finds himself being lifted off the ground and up into the air . . . "It must be magic!" he gasps. "This sandal will take me wherever I want to go!" Drifting higher, Rupert soon reaches the edge of Nutwood forest. "Amazing!" he gasps as he looks down to see the trees spread out below, like a huge, green carpet . . . As Rupert turns round he suddenly spots a distant figure. "There's somebody else up here!" he blinks. "They can fly as well!"

Rupert calls across the treetops to the distant figure, who spins round in surprise, then hurries over to join him. At first he thinks it must be Jack Frost but, as the boy gets nearer, Rupert sees it is a stranger, dressed in a colourful costume trimmed with feathers . . . "Hello!" he smiles. "You've found my sandal!" "Yes," nods Rupert. "I hope you don't mind me trying it out." "No!" laughs the boy. "I can still fly with one shoe but I never thought that anyone else would learn the same trick!"

The boy asks Rupert where they are –
"Are you from Nutwood? Is it far?"

"My cousin Jack comes every year,
He thought that I might like it here . . ."

"Come on!" the Skylark gives a cry.
"It's fun to play when you can fly!"

He swoops to earth and grabs a stick –
"Just what we need to play a trick . . ."

"Do you live in Nutwood?" asks the boy. "Yes," says Rupert. "I was crossing the common when I found your sandal . . ." "It must have fallen off while I was practising summersaults!" laughs Rupert's new friend. "I flew here with the birds! My cousin said I'd like it. He comes to Nutwood to collect your snowmen . . ." "Snowmen?" blinks Rupert. "But that must be Jack Frost!" "That's right!" nods the boy. "I'm his cousin, Skylark. I live near the equator, where your birds go in the winter . . ."

Now that he has found the sandal's owner, Rupert offers to return it straightaway . . . "No, no!" laughs Skylark. "You won't be able to fly if you take it off. I've come to Nutwood to have some fun. There are all sorts of games we can play if we can both fly . . ." Swooping down towards Nutwood's lake, he picks up a fallen branch with a whoop of delight. "Perfect!" he cries. "I'll show you how to write on water!" "Water?" blinks Rupert. "Follow me!" calls Skylark. "Over the lake . . ."

RUPERT WALKS A TIGHTROPE

The boy starts drawing on the lake –
"Look, Rupert! It's a watersnake!"

"We'll try a new game now! Let's see . . .
That clothes-line will do perfectly!"

"It's time to learn a new trick now –
Tightrope walking! I'll show you how . . ."

"Just don't look down! You're doing fine!"
He calls as Rupert walks the line.

As Rupert looks on, Skylark hovers over the surface of the lake and stirs the water with the tip of his stick . . . "Amazing!" gasps Rupert. "I can see what you're drawing!" "A watersnake!" laughs the boy as Nutwood's ducks flap their wings. "Now let's find a new game to play." Flying towards Nutwood, he catches sight of Mrs. Sheep's cottage. "Look at that clothes-line!" Skylark chuckles. "The garden's empty. No-one's about. It's too good to miss . . ." "What do you mean?" blinks Rupert.

To Rupert's surprise, Skylark flies down to Mrs. Sheep's garden and starts skipping along the washing-line, like a tightrope walker . . . "Come on!" he cries. "You should be able to do this too, now you can fly." Rupert puts one foot on the line, then steps forward gingerly . . . "Don't look down!" calls Skylark. "Just follow me across. You'll soon get the hang of it!" "You're right!" laughs Rupert. "No wonder you like playing games! If I could fly, I'd be able to do tricks like this all the time!"

RUPERT'S PAL PLANS A NEW TRICK

*"Bless me!" blinks Mrs. Sheep. "You two
Are flying! No, it can't be true . . ."*

*The Skylark hurries on his way –
"A farm! Now **that's** the place to play!"*

*"Oh, dear!" thinks Rupert anxiously . . .
"Whatever will his next trick be?"*

*"A weathercock!" the Skylark cries.
"Let's find out how well this one flies . . ."*

Just as Rupert gets to the end of the washing line, he suddenly hears somebody call his name . . . "Rupert!" cries Mrs. Sheep. "Fancy you being able to walk the tightrope! I couldn't believe my eyes!" "I hope you don't mind us using your clothes line . . ." starts Rupert but Skylark is already over the hedge and off in search of new adventures. "Wait!" calls Rupert as he hurries after his new chum. "Come on!" cries Skylark. "I can see a farm. There'll be lots to do there . . ."

Rupert chases after Skylark, anxiously wondering what he plans to get up to at Farmer Brown's . . . "A weathercock!" the prankster cries. "I *knew* we'd find one somewhere!" It is a quiet day and the farm seems deserted as the pair hover up above the rooftops. "Farmer Brown must be out on his rounds," thinks Rupert, with a sign of relief. "Have you ever seen a weathercock fly?" asks Skylark. "No," says Rupert. "I thought they stayed where they were." "Not always!" smiles the Lark.

RUPERT SEES A WEATHERCOCK FLY

"We'll see who spins the tin bird best –
Through four points – North, South, East and West!"

The cockerel spins so violently
It leaves its old perch and breaks free . . .

"Oh, no!" gasps Rupert in dismay –
"The weathercock's flying away!"

But Skylark doesn't seem to care –
He's off to try another dare . . .

"Watch!" calls Skylark. "We'll have a competition to see who can make it go fastest . . ." Seizing the weathercock by the tail, he spins it round as if a hurricane was blowing. "Stop!" cries Rupert. "You'll make it dizzy!" "Nonsense!" laughs his companion. "They're *meant* to go round and round . . ." As he speaks, the weathercock suddenly breaks free from its perch and shoots up into the air. "Now look what you've done!" gasps Rupert. "Gosh!" blinks Skylark. "I've never seen that before!"

To Rupert's amazement the weathercock gives an angry squawk, flaps its metal wings and flies off over the fields . . . "It's leaving!" he gasps. "Farmer Brown will be furious when he finds out what has happened!" "Farmer Brown?" asks Skylark. "Is he the man walking past the barn?" "Yes . . ." groans Rupert. "If he sees the weathercock flying off it will make things even worse!" "Don't fuss!" says Skylark. "Silly old farmers don't worry me! Let's see if he wants to join the fun!"

RUPERT'S PAL TEASES THE FARMER

"Hats off!" cries Skylark, swooping down
To play a trick on Farmer Brown . . .

"What fun!" he laughs. "Did you see that?
Now, what shall we do with this hat?"

"Scamp!" calls the farmer angrily.
"Just throw that hat back down to me!"

The hat lands on its owner's head –
"Let's find another game instead!"

"Hats off!" cries Skylark, swooping down towards Farmer Brown. To Rupert's horror, he snatches the farmer's hat and flies up with a whoop. At first, Farmer Brown thinks his hat has been blown off by the wind. He looks round, then catches sight of Rupert and Skylark, hovering over his head . . . "Rupert!" he cries. "What's going on? Who's that holding my hat?" "What fun!" laughs Skylark. "Now, where shall I put this? Perhaps the treetops? We could see how long it takes to blow down . . ."

"Give back that hat, you scallywag!" calls Farmer Brown. "I don't mind a joke but you've gone too far . . ." "All right!" says the prankster. "Stand still and I'll see what I can do!" Taking careful aim, he throws the hat down towards the farmer, like a ring at a hoop-la stall. "Bull's-eye!" he laughs as it lands on Farmer Brown's head. "You can't complain about that, can you? Come on, Rupert. Let's go and find something else to play. There's lots of Nutwood I haven't seen yet!"

RUPERT'S FRIENDS ARE ANNOYED

"A football match! Let's join in too!
Your friends won't mind if I'm with you . . ."

The pals are all astonished by
The figure swooping from the sky . . .

"Catch!" calls the Skylark. "We can throw
The ball between us – to and fro . . ."

But Rupert flies back down to where
His startled pals all stand and stare.

Leaving the farm behind them, Rupert and Skylark fly over Nutwood Common until they spot a group of chums playing football . . . "That looks fun!" says the visitor. "Do you think they'll mind if I join in?" "Of course not," says Rupert. "Although we'd better land out of sight so they aren't too startled . . ." "Land?" laughs Skylark. "But that would spoil the game . . ." As Rupert looks on, his companion swoops down and catches the ball in mid-air. "Hey!" gasps Algy. "What's the big idea?"

"Catch!" calls Skylark, throwing the pals' ball to Rupert. "We'll have a game of Piggy in the Middle . . ." "No you won't!" cries Algy. "Give us back our ball! Come on, Rupert! I don't know who your new friend is, but I don't think much of his manners . . ." "Sorry!" says Rupert, drifting down to join his chums. "He was only having fun. I'm sure he didn't *mean* to spoil your game . . ." "You're flying too!" blinks Willie. "What's going on? It must be magic! Or are we all dreaming?"

RUPERT CHASES SKYLARK

"This boy's called Skylark, everyone –
He likes to play jokes and have fun . . ."

"Come on!" calls Skylark. "Time to play!"
He snatches Rupert's scarf away . . .

"Hey!" Rupert calls. "Give that to me!"
The boy just gives a cry of glee . . .

He flies off high above the ground
Towards an ancient tower he's found . . .

Handing Algy the ball, Rupert tells his chums the whole story of how he found the winged sandal, then met its mischievous owner . . . "He's called Skylark," Rupert explains. "And he loves playing jokes and pranks! At first it was fun, but the trouble is, he just doesn't know when to stop . . ." As Rupert speaks, he suddenly feels someone tugging at his scarf. "Come on!" laughs Skylark. "Don't be a spoilsport! Let's play something else. How about Hide and Seek?"

"Hey! Come back with my scarf!" calls Rupert. "Catch me if you can!" laughs Skylark, bounding off over the fields. "Come back!" cries Rupert, but the boy flies over the treetops, trailing the scarf behind. "I'd better not let him out of sight!" thinks Rupert. As the pair reach the edge of the common, Skylark spots the Old Professor's tower. "Oh, no!" groans Rupert. "I hope there aren't any windows open. If he gets his hands on one of the Professor's machines, who knows *what* might happen?"

RUPERT ASTONISHES BODKIN

"Come on!" calls Skylark. "Now let's see
How fast you are. Catch up with me!"

"Wait! Skylark!" Rupert gives a shout
As Bodkin happens to look out . . .

"Amazing!" Bodkin blinks. "I'm sure
I've never seen you fly before!"

Rupert starts to explain, but then
The Skylark flies off once again.

As the pair near the Professor's tower, Skylark glances over his shoulder and catches sight of Rupert. "Come on, slowcoach!" he calls. "You'll never catch me like that!" Before Rupert can answer, his new pal disappears from sight behind the ivy-clad building. "You'll have to be quick to catch me!" calls the boy. "My next hiding place will be *much* harder to find." As Rupert circles round the tower, an astonished Bodkin appears at the window and looks out to see who's there . . .

"Rupert!" cries Bodkin. "I thought I heard your voice. "What are you doing?" "Chasing someone!" calls Rupert. "I can't stop to explain or they'll get away . . ." "He's flying too!" gasps Bodkin. "I've never seen anything like it!" Leaving the tower behind, Rupert follows Skylark over the fields surrounding Nutwood and up towards a ridge of rocky hills. "I wonder where he's heading for?" he murmurs. "If we keep going this way we'll end up by the coast. I do hope Skylark stops soon . . ."

RUPERT FINDS SKYLARK

As Rupert thinks he's drawing near,
The Skylark seems to disappear!

"He's hiding!" Rupert thinks, "But where?
I know! I'll try that nest, up there . . ."

"Well done!" laughs Skylark. "Let's see how
You get on – hiding from me now . . ."

But, suddenly, an eagle flies
Towards the nest. "Help!" Skylark cries.

Suddenly, as Rupert chases after him, Skylark seems to vanish . . . "I wonder where he's gone?" Rupert thinks. "He must be hiding somewhere. Perhaps at the top of one of those tall trees . . ." Rupert searches the tree-tops carefully, but, to his surprise, there is no sign of the prankster to be seen. "What now?" Rupert sighs. "I can't fly back to Nutwood and leave him behind . . ." Just then, the sound of giggling breaks the silence. "Skylark!" thinks Rupert. "He must be in that empty nest . . ."

"Here I am!" laughs Skylark, popping up from the nest. "I was beginning to think you'd never find me . . ." "I didn't know we'd started!" says Rupert. "I suppose it's my turn to hide now?" "That's right!" says his friend. "I'll close my eyes and count to one hundred. You'll have to choose well though, Hide and Seek is one of my favourite games!" Just then, a shadow sweeps over the nest and a huge eagle swoops down towards the startled pair. "Help!" cries Skylark, but it is too late . . .

RUPERT SEES SKYLARK CARRIED OFF

The bird swoops down to seize its prey,
Then carries Rupert's chum away!

"Wait!" Skylark calls. "I didn't know
It was your nest. Please let me go!"

The bird speeds off as Rupert tries
To keep an eye on where it flies . . .

He sees the eagle gaining height,
Then cloud banks hide the bird from sight!

With an angry cry, the giant eagle seizes Skylark and lifts him out of the nest . . . Clutching him in its mighty talons, it flaps its wings and soars up into the sky. "Wait!" calls the boy. "I didn't know it was your nest! We were only playing a game!" Ignoring his protests, the great bird flies on, over the tree-tops towards the distant hills. "Don't worry!" calls Rupert. "I'm sure it will let you go soon. Perhaps it thinks you're some sort of baby bird.."

Rupert follows the eagle away from Nutwood and over the rocky hills. "I wonder where it's taking Skylark?" he thinks. "I'll try to keep as close as I can, so I see where it goes . . ." To Rupert's surprise, the great bird starts to climb higher and higher, up towards the clouds. "Perhaps it doesn't live here at all!" he thinks. "The nest might belong to another bird . . ." Next moment, the bird is lost from sight as it soars above a heavy bank of cloud, leaving Rupert far below . . .

RUPERT VISITS THE BIRD KING

The eagle soars through clouds to fly
Towards a castle in the sky . . .

"The Bird King's Palace!" Rupert blinks.
"They've gone to see the King!" he thinks.

"The weathercock! I might have known
*That **this** is where it would have flown . . ."*

The King says, "I take a dim view
Of people playing tricks, like you . . ."

Climbing higher and higher, Rupert passes through a misty patch of cloud then suddenly spots the towers of a castle in the sky. "Of course!" he gasps. "That's where the eagle's heading for! He's taking Skylark to the Bird King's palace . . ." Although Rupert has visited the palace before, the birds are clearly astonished to see him hovering in mid-air. "Can you take me to the King?" he asks as they fly round excitedly. "I think he has just had some other visitors from Nutwood . . ."

As Rupert lands in the castle courtyard, he can see Skylark being questioned by the King, with the eagle looking on sternly. "The weathercock's there too!" he gasps. "It must have flown straight from Nutwood to complain about being spun round!" "These are serious charges!" the King declares as Rupert draws near. "Your winged sandals make you a particular menace to creatures of the air. I shall have to send a formal complaint to your mother. It might be better if you were grounded for good!"

RUPERT ASKS FOR MERCY

"Wait!" Rupert calls. "Your Majesty,
"Don't act until you've heard my plea . . ."

"I know that Skylark caused alarm,
But all his high jinks meant no harm."

A parrot speaks for Skylark too –
"A harmless prankster, Sire! It's true!"

The King agrees to let things go –
"No more wild jokes from now on, though!

"Wait!" calls Rupert, interrupting the King. "Please don't be too harsh on him . . ." "Rupert?" blinks the toucan. "You *know* this miscreant? You may speak on his behalf, if you wish, but the charges against him are very grave!" "I know!" says Rupert. "Skylark has done a lot of bad things, but I'm sure he didn't mean any harm." "Really?" says the King. "I take a dim view of people who play pranks on weathercocks, not to mention trespassing in other birds' nests . . ."

As Rupert is talking to the King, a brightly coloured parrot flies up to join them. "Please, sire!" it squawks. "I can vouch for Skylark too! He lives in the forests of the South, with birds and animals as his play-fellows. He's a bit boisterous sometimes, but I know he'd never harm another creature!" "Well, well!" murmurs the King. "This does rather change things . . ." Turning to Skylark, he announces a Royal Pardon for past misdemeanours. "We'll let you make a fresh start!"

RUPERT'S PAL IS FORGIVEN

"I'm sorry for the harm I've done!
I'll make it up to everyone . . ."

The boy declares he'd like to stay
In Nutwood for another day . . .

The weathercock befriends the pair –
"It's been fun, taking to the air."

He shows the chums which way to go –
"Directions are my job, you know!"

Thanking the King, Skylark turns to the weathercock and apologises for spinning it off its perch . . . "I won't do it again!" he promises. "Good!" says the bird. "In that case, we can all be friends . . ." As the weathercock speaks, Skylark has a sudden idea. "I'd like to go back to Nutwood, if you don't mind," he tells the King. "There's something else I have to do before I go home . . ." "Very well," agrees the King. "You can all fly there together, with the weathercock as your guide . . ."

As soon as they have said goodbye to the King, Rupert and Skylark take to the air, together with the weathercock. "What an adventure!" it laughs. "It's the first time I've left Nutwood for years! Suppose I've got *you* to thank for that, young man!" Skylark is amazed by how quickly the bird finds its way back to Nutwood. "Easy, when you know how!" it preens. "North, South, East, West. Finding the way is what I do best! All you have to do is fly in the right direction . . ."

"We're home!" the cock crows in delight
As Nutwood's fields come into sight . . .

It flies back to its perch and then
Sits motionless and still again!

Skylark flies on until he comes
Across a group of Rupert's chums . . .

"Hello!" he smiles. "I've come to see
If you'd all like to play with me!"

Following the weathercock over hills and fields, Rupert and Skylark finally come to the outskirts of Nutwood and Farmer Brown's barn . . . "Goodbye!" calls their guide. "I'd better get back now, before I'm missed!" Flying down to the farm, it perches above the wind-vane and folds its wings. "Just like it was before!" laughs Skylark. "I never knew they could really fly . . ." "Me neither!" says Rupert. "I don't suppose I'd ever have found out if it hadn't been for you . . ."

Leaving the farm, Skylark flies on across Nutwood Common until he spots a group of Rupert's chums. "They're the reason I've come back," he says. "I want to make up for spoiling their game of football . . ." At first, the pals are rather wary of Rupert's companion, but when they hear that he wants to be friends, they soon agree to let bygones be bygones. "I wish *I* could fly like you!" says Bill. "You can!" laughs Skylark. "All you have to do is borrow one of my sandals . . ."

RUPERT'S CHUMS TRY FLYING TOO

The chums each take a turn to try
The magic shoes which make you fly . . .

"It's fun to play with friends, like you,
I wish I lived in Nutwood too!"

All Rupert's pals thank Skylark for
The game and ask him back once more . . .

"Goodbye!" calls Rupert. "For today –
I'm sure you'll soon be back this way!"

To the chums' delight, Skylark offers them a chance to try his sandals too . . . "You'll soon get the hang of flying!" he smiles. "It's amazing!" laughs Bill. "I feel as though I'm swimming through air . . ." "Watch me!" cries Algy. "My turn next!" calls Willie Mouse. "I'm glad they're enjoying themselves!" Skylark tells Rupert. "It must be nice to have so many friends . . ." "Haven't you?" asks Rupert. "No!" sighs the boy. "Birds, and monkeys sometimes, but no-one like you!"

At last, the fun ends and the pals return the magic sandals . . . "Thank you for coming back!" says Willie. "I hope you'll visit us again . . ." "Do you think I could?" says Skylark happily. "That would be marvellous!" "Of course!" smiles Rupert. "You can visit Nutwood whenever you like." "I will!" laughs the boy. "And now, I'd better be on my way! Thanks, everyone!" "Goodbye!" calls Rupert as Skylark sets off. "See you soon . . ."

THE END

Rupert's Chums

Look carefully at these pictures of Rupert's chums. Using the printed letters as clues, can you write their names on the grid below?

How carefully can you colour these two pictures?

John Harrold

Odd One Out

Look carefully at these drawings of Bingo, Rika and a Pippin. Sort them into matching pairs and put a circle round the odd ones out.

Who am I?

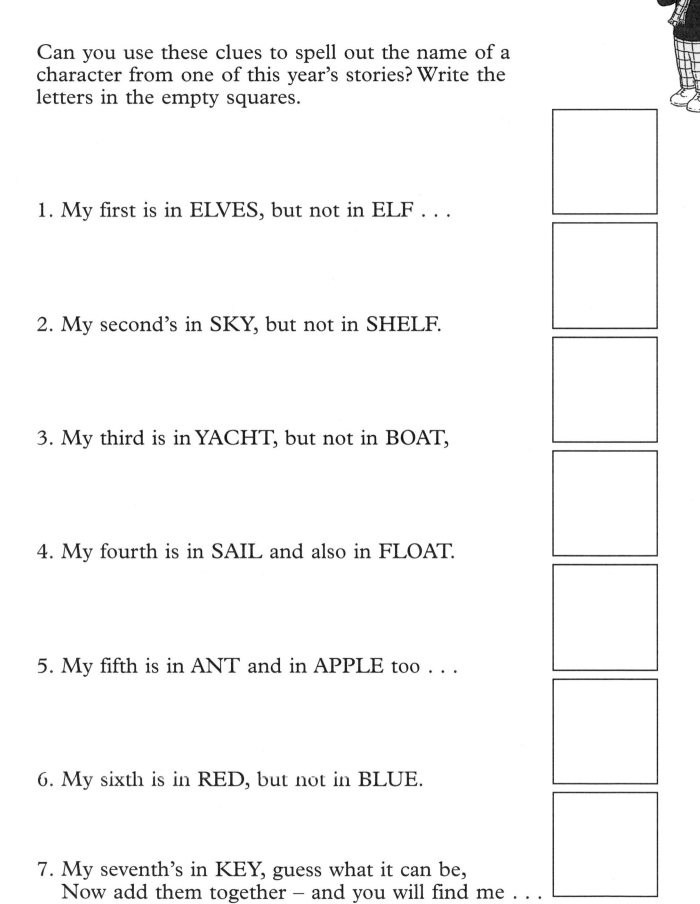

Can you use these clues to spell out the name of a character from one of this year's stories? Write the letters in the empty squares.

1. My first is in ELVES, but not in ELF . . .

2. My second's in SKY, but not in SHELF.

3. My third is in YACHT, but not in BOAT,

4. My fourth is in SAIL and also in FLOAT.

5. My fifth is in ANT and in APPLE too . . .

6. My sixth is in RED, but not in BLUE.

7. My seventh's in KEY, guess what it can be,
   Now add them together – and you will find me . . .

Answer on page 109

These two pictures look identical, but there are ten differences between them.
Can you spot them all? *Answers on page 109*

RUPERT
and the Apple Trees

John Harrold.

RUPERT'S PAL GETS A WARNING

One morning Rupert hears a cry,
"It's Podgy calling me, but why?"

"Stop!" Farmer Brown calls. "Come back here!"
"Help!" Podgy wails. "He's getting near!"

"Podgy!" cries Farmer Brown. "I'm sure
You stole some fruit and broke the law!"

"No!" Podgy wails. "It wasn't me!
I didn't climb a single tree . . ."

One autumn morning, Rupert is walking across Nutwood Common when he suddenly hears somebody calling his name . . . "It's Podgy!" he thinks, "I wonder what's wrong? He looks as if he might need help!" "Rupert!" gasps Podgy. "Run for your life! The farmer's coming! He's chased me all the way from the orchard!" Sure enough, Rupert spots an angry Farmer Brown, running after Podgy as fast as he can. "Come back here, Podgy Pig!" he bellows. "I want a word with you . . ."

Farmer Brown is so cross that he hardly seems to notice Rupert. "Podgy!" he cries. "I've had enough of your greedy scrumping. Any more and I'll have to have words with Constable Growler!" "But I wasn't!" protests Podgy. "I only took a short cut . . ." "To *look* at the apples, I suppose!" growls the farmer. "One of you lads has been scrumping in my orchard, that's for sure. I found a branch broken off the oldest tree and twigs all over the ground. It's got to stop, or there'll be trouble!"

*"I didn't have a chance to take
His fruit! It's all a big mistake!"*

*"If Podgy wasn't scrumping then
The apple thief might strike again . . ."*

*When Rupert gets home, Mr. Bear
Is looking at the apples there . . .*

*"There isn't time this afternoon,
But we should pick our harvest soon!"*

"What a fuss!" says Podgy as Farmer Brown turns on his heel and marches off. "I wouldn't mind, but I really *haven't* been scrumping apples! I was just about to start when Farmer Brown saw me . . ." Rupert warns his chum to stay out of the orchard until things have calmed down. "Don't worry!" says Podgy. "I won't even go near the farm for the next few days!" "If Podgy hasn't been scrumping apples, I wonder who has?" thinks Rupert. "Probably Freddy and Ferdy! I'd better warn them too . . ."

When Rupert gets home, Mr. Bear is out in the garden looking at *his* apple trees . . . "It's nearly time to harvest our crop!" he declares. "Perhaps you could give me a hand at the weekend?" Rupert agrees and remembers how delicious home-grown apples always taste. "That's because they're so fresh!" smiles his father. "Come on, you two!" calls Mrs. Bear. "It's time for tea. I'd better get my bottling jars ready if you're about to start picking apples . . ."

RUPERT SEES STRANGE LIGHTS

When Rupert goes to bed that night
He spots two tiny points of light . . .

"They look like lanterns," Rupert blinks.
"I'm sure I saw them move!" he thinks.

As he gets closer, Rupert sees
Two figures in the apple trees . . .

"Look out!" calls one as he gets near.
"We're not alone! There's someone here . . ."

Later in the evening, as Rupert gets ready for bed, he looks out into the garden and notices something strange. "I can see lights in one of the apple trees!" he gasps. "They look just like fireflies . . ." Hurrying downstairs, he opens the back door and steps outside. The lights are still there, glowing in the darkness like tiny lanterns. "How peculiar!" thinks Rupert as he walks silently towards the tree. "The lights are still moving. They seem to be going from branch to branch . . ."

As Rupert gets nearer to the apple trees he sees that the moving lights *are* tiny lanterns, held by Elf-like creatures with pointed hats . . . "They're looking for something!" he thinks. "I wonder what it can be?" Creeping forward, Rupert reaches the first tree and peers up at one of the little men. Before he can say anything, the Elf spins round with a cry of alarm. "Jonathan!" he calls. "There's somebody here . . ." "Don't worry!" says Rupert. "I'm sorry if I startled you . . ."

Who can the little green men be?
Why are they in the apple tree?

"We're Pippins!" cries the first. "We find
Gold apples of a special kind . . ."

"Each tree bears one gold fruit. We know
That its pips are the best to grow . . ."

As Rupert talks, the little pair
Hear someone call – It's Mrs. Bear!

Rupert is puzzled by the little men. At first, they look like Imps or Autumn Elves, but as he looks more closely he sees that they are dressed quite differently, in shades of green from head to toe . . . "Who are you?" he asks. "I hope you haven't been raiding Farmer Brown's orchard!" "No!" laughs the little man. "We're Pippins, not scrumpers! My name's Bramley and he's called Jonathan . . ." "What are you looking for?" asks Rupert. "A golden apple!" calls Jonathan. "There's one on every tree, you know!"

To Rupert's amazement, the Pippins say they collect golden apples from every tree they visit. "They have the best pips for planting!" explains Jonathan. "We use them all to bring on new trees . . ." "I've never noticed golden apples before," says Rupert. "No!" nods Bramley. "We normally pick them early." "This year's different!" his companion sighs. "Someone else has been gathering golden apples too! Farmer Brown's orchard is almost bare!" Just then, the door opens and Mrs. Bear calls Rupert's name . . .

"Who's there?" asks Mrs. Bear, but then
The Pippins have both gone again . . .

"Come in!" she smiles. "You sleepy head!
It's time you were tucked up in bed . . ."

Next morning, Rupert hurries out
To see if Pippins are about . . .

As Rupert nears the orchard he
Spots Freddy, climbing up a tree!

"Do I hear voices?" asks Mrs. Bear. "Who are you talking to?" "Pippins!" says Rupert. "I found them in our apple tree . . ." He turns back to show Bramley and Jonathan to his mother but the glowing lanterns have gone and the garden is completely deserted. "Come in!" she smiles. "It's too late to play games outside now." "But they *were* here," gasps Rupert. "I saw them, really! Collecting golden apples from each tree . . ." "Rupert!" says Mrs. Bear. "There'll be plenty of time to play tomorrow!"

Next morning, Rupert decides to go and ask Odmedod the scarecrow if *he* knows anything about the Pippins . . . "He's bound to have seen them gathering apples in Farmer Brown's orchard!" he thinks. "I wonder if he knows where they live?" On the way to the farm, Rupert suddenly notices somebody climbing a tree in the lower orchard. "Freddy Fox!" he blinks. "And there's Ferdy, waiting down below. So they *have* been scrumping apples, while poor old Podgy got the blame!"

RUPERT WARNS THE FOXES

"Look out!" warns Rupert. "Hurry down.
You'll both be caught by Farmer Brown!"

"Don't worry! He can have the rest –
These yellow apples taste the best!"

Just then, the Foxes hear a yell –
The farmer's spotted them as well . . .

"Run!" Ferdy calls. The Foxes flee
As Farmer Brown shouts angrily.

Rupert scrambles into the orchard and runs across to warn the Foxes. "Farmer Brown's on the warpath!" he gasps. "There'll be trouble if he spots you scrumping apples . . ." "He won't mind!" laughs Ferdy. "We're only picking *one* apple from each tree!" "These yellowy ones taste much better than all the others," says Freddy. "I've never noticed them before, but they're really delicious!" "Yellow?" blinks Rupert. "But those are the golden apples the Pippins need!"

"Pippins?" asks Freddy. "Who are they? They can't have our apples anyway!" Rupert is about to explain, when he hears an angry cry . . . "Farmer Brown!" gasps Ferdy, dropping his sack. "Run for it!" shouts his brother. The pair take to their heels, with the farmer in hot pursuit. "He didn't see me!" thinks Rupert. "I must have been hidden behind this bush." Keeping out of sight, he decides to wait till the farmer has gone. By his side lies the Fox brothers' sack, filled with golden apples . . .

RUPERT SAVES THE SPECIAL APPLES

"The Foxes' apples!" Rupert blinks.
"They've left them all behind!" he thinks . . .

Just then he hears a Pippin call,
"Phew! That was close! I saw it all!"

The Pippin smiles to find out how
The yellow fruit's been gathered now . . .

"We'll take it to the Nursery!
I'll lead the way. You follow me!"

As Farmer Brown disappears after the Foxes, Rupert picks up the sack of apples and wonders what to do next. "Hello!" calls a voice. "That was a close run thing! You're lucky the farmer didn't see you!" Looking up, Rupert spots a little figure peering down from the branches of a nearby tree. "One of the Pippins!" he blinks. "That's right!" smiles the little man. "I'm Jonathan. We met last night. I've come to have a final look in Farmer Brown's orchard . . ."

When Rupert explains how the Foxes have been gathering golden apples, the Pippin is overjoyed. "They've done my work for me!" he laughs. "There are enough here to grow a hundred trees. All we have to do is get them to the Nursery . . ." "Nursery?" asks Rupert. "Yes!" says the Pippin. "It's where we grow new trees. After all you've done to help, I'm sure the others won't mind if you come too." Intrigued to find out more, Rupert follows Jonathan through the trees, across the orchard.

*"This way!" the Pippin calls. "I'll show
You something only Pippins know . . ."*

*"A door!" blinks Rupert. "Now I see . . .
Each Pippin has a special key!"*

*"Like Imps and Elves we move around
Through secret tunnels underground!"*

*"You'll soon see where the others are!"
The Pippin calls. "It isn't far . . ."*

Leading Rupert to the edge of the orchard, the Pippin stops suddenly by a tangle of bushes. "I'm about to show you a secret!" he says, "Stay close behind me and keep down low . . ." Pushing his way forward, Jonathan reveals a tiny doorway in the wall, completely hidden by a mass of leaves. "It's a short-cut!" he smiles. "Elves and Imps use it too, but Farmer Brown doesn't even know it's here!" Taking a key from his pocket, the Pippin unlocks the door and pushes it open for Rupert to enter . . .

On the other side of the door, Rupert is surprised to find a rocky tunnel, leading underground . . . "I thought we were going to another orchard," he blinks. "We are!" laughs his guide. "This is a special pathway between our orchard and Farmer Brown's." "I wonder how far it goes?" thinks Rupert as he follows the Pippin. "I've never really thought about the far side of the orchard. I suppose we'll come out somewhere near the middle of Nutwood Forest . . ."

"We're nearly there now! Can you see?
A glimpse of daylight! Follow me . . . "

"Another orchard!" Rupert cries.
*"It's **full** of Pippins! What a size . . . "*

"Look, everybody! We've come back
With yellow apples in our sack!"

"The Apple Cart! Let's see if he
Will take us to the Nursery . . . "

Carrying the sack of golden apples, Rupert follows Jonathan along a winding tunnel that seems to go on and on for miles . . . "Nearly there!" calls the Pippin cheerfully. "There! You can see the end. We won't be long now!" Emerging into the sunshine, Rupert is amazed to see a huge orchard, filled with Pippins, all busily picking apples from the trees. "Harvest time!" says Jonathan. "It's a busy month for us! Follow me and I'll take you to see the Nurseries . . . "

The other Pippins are astonished to see an unexpected visitor. "We've brought the golden apples from Farmer Brown's!" explains Jonathan. "They're needed in the Nursery straightaway." "The Nursery?" asks one of the harvesters. "You're just in time! There's an Apple Cart about to leave with a full load. Hurry along and you can hitch a ride!" Jonathan runs to a grassy clearing where a horse and cart stand waiting. "Hello, there!" he calls. "Don't go yet! We'd like to come too . . . "

RUPERT MEETS THE CHIEF GARDENER

The cart moves off and Rupert sees
Some buildings set amongst the trees . . .

The Pippin hurries off to tell
The Gardener that all is well . . .

The Pippins' Chief is pleased at all
The golden apples – "What a haul!"

"Please stay for lunch and let us show
You what we do, before you go . . . "

To Rupert's delight, the driver of the Apple Cart turns out to be Bramley, the other Pippin he met in the garden. "Climb up!" he smiles. "Everyone *will* be pleased you've got the goldens!" As the cart trundles across the orchard, Rupert spots a cluster of buildings, grouped around some glass-houses ... "The Nursery!" announces Jonathan. He hops down and hurries off to tell the Chief Gardener the news. "Old Laxton!" nods Bramley. "He's in charge of all our new trees . . ."

The Chief Gardener is delighted to see Rupert's sack of golden apples. "Just what we need!" he cries. "Each pip will grow into a little seedling and, in time, there'll be plenty of new trees to keep the orchards going . . ." When he hears how he has helped the Pippins, the Chief invites Rupert to stay for a while and have a closer look at the Nursery. "Jonathan will show you round," he says. "The other Pippins are just about to have lunch. Why don't you two go and join them?"

RUPERT HAS A TOFFEE APPLE

*The Pippins' menu shows that they
Eat apple dishes every day!*

*"Each apple's different! Our cooks know
What's best for every type we grow . . . "*

*"There's one more thing you ought to see . . .
Our toffee apple factory!"*

*"The ones that we don't eat are sold
To shops, like Nutwood's!" Rupert's told . . .*

Rupert follows Jonathan into the Pippins' canteen. When he looks at the menu, he sees that everything on it is made from apples! "They're our favourite food!" says Jonathan. "It's amazing what you can do with apples. We grow everything here – from pearmains to pimpernels!" "Toffee-apples!" laughs Rupert. "My friend Podgy loves those!" "Try one!" says the Pippin. "They're from this morning's batch. I'll show you how they're made, if you like. The toffee's a special recipe we invented ourselves!"

When Rupert has finished lunch, his guide leads him along a path towards another building. The air is suddenly filled with a strong, sweet smell which wafts towards them. "Toffee!" smiles Jonathan. Rupert follows him into a busy kitchen, where Pippins are dipping apples into a bubbling vat, then standing them to cool on trays. "We make a fresh batch every day," he explains. "Those we don't eat are packaged up and sold to shops. Your friend Podgy must be one of our best customers!"

RUPERT GETS AN INVITATION

As Rupert walks along he sees
A picture of some apple trees . . .

"Wassailing's when we stay out late –
Come too and help us celebrate!"

The Pippins wait till twilight, then
Set out towards the trees again . . .

"Stay close to us and use your light!"
Says Bramley. "Don't get lost at night!"

As Rupert is taken to see how juice is made at the apple press, he catches sight of a poster on the wall... "Grand Wassailing!" he reads. "That's tonight!" says Jonathan. "We're going to water the trees with a special tonic. It's a sort of thank-you for all the apples they've given us. We sing songs as well and celebrate the autumn's harvest." "What fun!" laughs Rupert. "Do you go to Farmer Brown's orchard?" "Of course!" nods Jonathan. "You can come too! We go when it's dark, so that nobody sees . . ."

The Pippins spend the rest of the afternoon getting ready for the Grand Wassailing . . . "We need enough tonic for the whole orchard!" explains Jonathan. "It only takes a few drops for each tree but there are hundreds to visit." As darkness falls, the Pippins light their lanterns and hand one to Rupert. "You'll need this!" says Bramley. "It's easy to get lost in the dark, so make sure you stay close to us." "Time to go!" calls Jonathan. "Wassailers join the Round!"

RUPERT SINGS WITH THE PIPPINS

The Pippins all stand in a ring
And wait until it's time to sing . . .

A horn blows and they all begin –
"Hurrah!" calls Rupert, joining in . . .

Now Rupert knows the Pippins' song,
He sings it as they march along . . .

"Our last tree! Now we've done them all
It's time to make another call . . . "

As Rupert joins the Pippins, he finds them gathered round the first tree in a big circle. "Ready, everyone?" asks Jonathan. Bramley nods and gestures to a third Pippin who blows a long, loud note on his horn. The others start to sing as Bramley sprays the tree with tonic. "Here's to thee, good apple tree. We thank you for the fruit we store. Caps full, sacks full. Holla! Holla! Hurrah!" Rupert laughs then joins them in a final chorus. "Holla! Holla! Hurrah!"

Moving from apple tree to apple tree, the Pippins spray each one with tonic and sing the same song over and over again. Before long, Rupert knows all the words and can join in from start to finish. "Caps full, sacks full. Holla! Holla! Hurrah!" When the Wassailers have been round the whole orchard, Jonathan leads them towards the clump of bushes which marks the start of the tunnel back to Nutwood. "This way, everyone!" he calls. "Our night's work isn't over yet!"

RUPERT JOINS A PROCESSION

"This way! There's still a lot to do!
We spray all Farmer Brown's trees too . . . "

"What fun!" thinks Rupert. "Now I know
What makes all Farmer Brown's trees grow!"

The Pippins march from tree to tree
And sing to each one cheerfully.

Then, finally, there's one last flask
Of tonic for a special task . . .

With their tiny lanterns shimmering in the gloom, the Pippins set off along the rocky tunnel towards Farmer Brown's orchard. "If only he knew!" laughs Rupert. "I am glad you asked me to come wassailing too!" "You're welcome!" says Jonathan. "If it hadn't been for your help, we would have lost Nutwood's golden apples and been short of seedlings to replant!" At the end of the tunnel Jonathan opens the door and leads the band of wassailers to the first of Farmer Brown's trees . . .

In Farmer Brown's orchard the Pippins sing their Wassailing song, blow their horn and spray tonic on every tree. "It will help them through the winter," explains Bramley. "Frost and fog, rain and snow, and hardly a ray of sunshine till Spring arrives! Poor trees! I feel chilly just thinking about it!" When the tour of the orchard has ended, the Pippins still have one bottle of tonic left over . . . "That's for our final call!" smiles Jonathan. "It's somewhere you should recognise!"

"My house!" laughs Rupert. "Now I see,
You've saved the last wassail for me!"

The Pippins start to sing their song
Then stop abruptly – something's wrong!

It's Mr. Bear! "Who's there?" he cries
And takes the Pippins by surprise . . .

"They've gone!" "Yes!" Rupert smiles. "But I
Can tell you what they do – and why . . ."

Rupert marches off along the lane, then laughs when he realises where the Pippins are going next. "My house!" he blinks. "That's right!" says Jonathan. "We've come to sing to *your* trees!" Handing Rupert the last bottle of tonic, he leads the Pippins in a rousing chorus while Rupert works the spray . . . They have just finished when the garden is suddenly flooded with light from the kitchen. "Somebody's coming!" gasps Bramley. "They must have seen the glint of our lanterns!"

"Hello!" calls Rupert's father. "You're out very late! What were all those lights I saw? Is there somebody here?" "There was!" smiles Rupert. "They've gone now, I'm afraid. Pippins don't like being seen . . ." "Pippins?" blinks Mr. Bear. "Apple Elves!" says Rupert. "We've been out wassailing!" "Really!" laughs his father, then spots Rupert's bottle. "Tree tonic!" beams Rupert. "Let's go inside and I'll tell you all about it . . ."

Rupert's Crossword Puzzle

See if you can complete this crossword. Most of the answers can be found in stories from this year's annual . . .

ACROSS

3. Precious metal (4)
5. Disc for throwing – from America (7)
6. Rupert's greedy chum (5)
8. Little man, Autumn figure (3)
11. "The brainy pup" – Rupert's clever pal (5)
14. Wicked Sultan (5)
18. Underground passage (6)
19. American law-officer (7)
22. Large-beaked bird – Royal (6)
24. Looked after by Pippins (5,5)
27. Rupert's pal – small and timid (6,5)
30. Supports a sail (4)
31. American coin (6)
33. Set free (7)
34. Metal bird – normally flightless (11)

DOWN

1. Jack Frost's cousin (5,8)
2. Used by Rika to call 23 down (4)
4. Country where Rika lives (7)
5. Ferdy Fox's brother (6)
7. Before today (9)
9. Seeker after 3 across (10)
10. Stop (3)
12. Rupert's American Uncle (7)
13. Machine used by 11 across to look for 3 across (5,8)
15. Nutwood's farmer (5)
16. December celebration (9)
17. Shines in the sky, hot (3)
20. Jolly, celebratory (7)
21. Gifts (8)
23. Northern animals, herded by Rika (8)
25. Desire, sometimes granted (4)
26. Eastern magician (6)
28. Little bird, rascal (7)
29. Falls from sky in winter (4)
30. What 17 down docs to 29 down (4)
31. Famous extinct bird (4)
32. Opposite of West (4)

Solution on page 109

Mrs. Bear's Apple Crumble

A delicious apple pudding which is easy to make . . .

INGREDIENTS

Crumble Topping:
4oz (100g) plain flour
3oz (75g) butter
2oz (50g) caster sugar
1oz (25g) porridge oats
pinch of salt

Apple Filling:
5 eating apples★
pinch of cinnamon
4 tablespoons of water

★*(Cooking apples can be used instead, if preferred. Use 3-4 large apples and add 2oz (50g) sugar to sweeten.)*

1. Pre-heat oven to 190 C (375 F), Gas Mark 5

2. Sieve flour into a large mixing bowl. Cut the butter into small pieces and using your finger tips rub into the flour. Add sugar, oats and salt and continue rubbing until the mixture forms large crumbs.

3. Peel and core the apples. Cut into slices. Place in a deep pie dish and add 4 tablespoons of water. (Don't forget to add 2oz (50g) of caster sugar if you are using cooking apples)

4. Cover the apples with the crumble mixture and press down lightly with the back of a tablespoon.

5. Bake in a pre-heated oven (190 C/375 F/Gas Mark 5) for 40-45 minutes, until apples are soft and topping is golden.

Another two pictures which look identical. There are actually nine differences between them. Can you spot them all? *Answers on page 109*

Pippins' Baked Apples

Another simple recipe – which uses cooking apples (Bramleys).

INGREDIENTS
One large cooking apple per person

For each apple:
1 dessertspoon of golden syrup
1 teaspoon of brown sugar
2 teaspoons of sultanas
A pinch of cinnamon
Small knob of butter

1. Pre-heat oven to 350F/180C/ Gas Mark 4.

2. Core the apples and prick their skins with a fork.

3. Mix the filling ingredients together in a bowl.

4. Place the apples in an ovenproof dish.

5. Spoon filling mixture into centre of each apple.

6. Pour four tablespoons of water around the apples.

7. Bake in a pre-heated over (350F/180C/Gas Mark 4) for about 50 minutes – until the apples are soft.

8. Spoon over melted syrup juice and serve with a little cream.

Which Story?

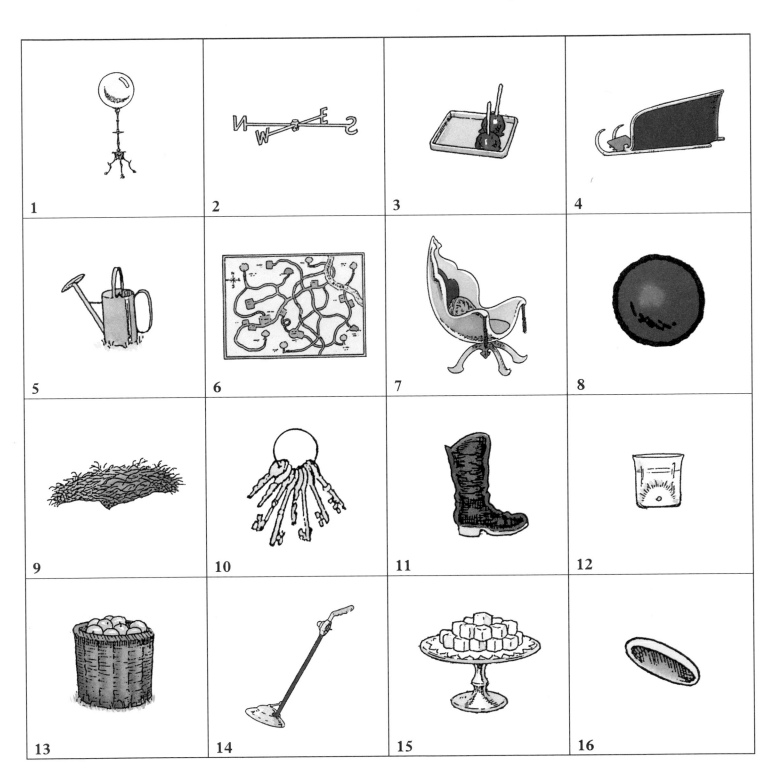

Each of the objects shown above appears in a story from this year's Annual.
Can you find out where they are from?

Answers on page 109

RUPERT and

*"It's nearly Christmas – time you wrote
To Santa, Rupert. Send a note . . ."*

Christmas is coming and Rupert is writing a list to Santa . . . "What I *really* want is a new bike!" he tells his mother. "That's rather big to fit on a sledge!" smiles Mrs. Bear. "Write down some other things too, then leave it for Santa to choose." Rupert does as she suggests, then hurries to post his letter. As he reaches the post-box, Bill Badger appears, carrying an envelope. "Hello!" he calls. "I hope I'm in time to send this to the North Pole!"

the Christmas List

*Bill Badger's written his list too –
"Good! I'll catch the same post as you . . ."*

*One morning, Mr. Bear is sure
He hears the postman at the door . . .*

A few days later, Rupert and his parents are discussing everything they have to do before Christmas. "Mince pies!" says Mr. Bear. "Of course!" laughs his wife. "But first, we'll write our Christmas cards." "I'll help to deliver them!" says Rupert. "I say!" blinks Mr. Bear. "That sounds like a delivery now . . ." Sure enough, a letter lies on the mat, with a postmark from the North Pole. "Look, Rupert!" smiles Mr. Bear. "It's addressed to you."

*"A letter, Rupert. Somebody
At the North Pole! Who could it be?"*

RUPERT GETS A STRANGE BILL

*"Oh, dear!" blinks Rupert in dismay.
"The letter says we have to pay!"*

*"It looks like someone's prank to me –
All Santa's gifts are always free!"*

*"It must be Bill! He sometimes tries
To trick his chums with a surprise . . ."*

*"No!" Bill declares. "I got one too!
I thought it was a joke from **you**!"*

Rupert opens the letter excitedly. At first he thinks it might be from his Uncle Polar, or perhaps Jack Frost, who lives near the Pole in a great ice palace. To his surprise, he sees the envelope contains a note from Santa, listing all the things he asked for, but with a set of prices added by the side. "It's a bill!" gasps Mr. Bear. "How odd!" blinks Rupert's mother. "Santa never charges for presents! It must be some sort of prank. I wonder if anyone else has been sent one too?"

Rupert wonders which of his chums might have sent him the note . . . "Bill Badger!" he laughs. "He must have had the idea when he saw me sending my list to Santa." Hurrying across the common, Rupert takes the letter with him to show his pal. To his surprise, Bill produces an identical envelope with a list of all the presents he asked for in *his* letter to Santa. "I thought you might have sent it as a joke!" he gasps. "The postmark says North Pole, so I suppose it really must be from Santa . . ."

RUPERT HEARS RIKA'S STORY

"It all seems so strange!" Rupert still
Can't get used to a Christmas bill . . .

Then, suddenly, he hears a cry
And spots a reindeer in the sky . . .

"It's Rika!" Rupert smiles. "What fun!
She's come to visit everyone . . ."

But Rika soon tells Rupert she
Needs help to solve a mystery . . .

As Rupert walks back from seeing his chum, he thinks about the bill from Santa and how expensive it will be. "I suppose I could just buy the football," he thinks. "But we might as well go to a shop in Nutchester for that . . ." Suddenly, he hears somebody calling his name. "Who's there?" he blinks looking all round. "Up here!" laughs a girl's voice. "Rika!" gasps Rupert, as a flying reindeer swoops down towards him with a familiar figure sitting on its back . . .

Rupert is delighted to see his friend from Lapland, who looks after Santa's reindeer. At first he thinks she must have come to visit Nutwood for fun, but as he hurries forward to say hello, he can see that she looks worried . . . "I've come to ask for help!" Rika explains. "Something very strange has happened to Santa's reindeer. I called them as usual but only Dancer came! All the others have vanished. I need to find them in time to pull Santa's sleigh."

RUPERT FLIES ON A REINDEER

*"**One** reindeer can't pull Santa's sleigh –*
I need the others straightaway!"

"Can I help Rika?" "Yes, but you
Will need to wear some warm clothes too . . ."

"Hold tight!" calls Rika. "Off we fly –
To Santa's castle in the sky!"

What will the pair find? Rupert still
Feels mystified by Santa's bill . . .

Rika tells Rupert that Santa's reindeer spend the summer months grazing with the rest of the herds in Lapland. "I call them at the start of December," she explains. "Then we all fly to Santa's castle . . ." "I wonder what can have happened to the others?" says Rupert. "*One* reindeer won't be enough to pull Santa's sleigh." The pair go to tell Rupert's mother what has happened and ask if he can help Rika with her search. "Of course!" says Mrs. Bear. "But don't forget to wrap up well . . ."

As soon as Rupert is ready to leave, Rika tells him to climb up behind her on Dancer. "To Santa's castle in the sky – please go as fast as you can fly . . ." The reindeer bounds forward and is soon soaring high over Nutwood and across the surrounding fields. "Missing reindeer aren't the only mystery," Rupert tells Rika as they fly along. "I'm sure that Santa wouldn't start charging everyone for presents . . ." "Certainly not!" says Rika. "That doesn't sound right at all."

RUPERT VISITS SANTA'S CASTLE

On Dancer flies – the pair catch sight
Of Santa's castle, bathed in light . . .

The flying reindeer starts to slow –
"Well done!" says Rika. "Down we go!"

"How strange!" says Rupert. "Nobody
Is to be seen. Where can they be?"

The puzzled chums both look around.
Then Rupert calls, "Look what I've found . . ."

As Rupert and Rika leave Nutwood behind them, they fly steadily North, until the air grows cold and the mountains are topped with snow. At Rika's command the reindeer starts to climb higher and higher until it reaches the clouds . . . "There's Santa's castle!" cries Rika. "Keep going Dancer, we're nearly there!" Rupert has visited Santa before, but still blinks in wonder at the gleaming turrets and towers. "Directly over the North Pole!" calls Rika. "That's how I know where to find it."

Swooping down towards the castle, the chums land gently in the courtyard. To Rupert's surprise, it seems completely deserted. "How odd!" blinks Rika. "There's nobody here at all!" "I thought Christmas was Santa's busiest time," says Rupert. "It is!" nods Rika. "Let's look around and see where everyone has gone." The pair are even more mystified to find Santa's sleigh standing all by itself in the empty courtyard. "I say!" hisses Rupert. "Come and look down here!"

RUPERT AND RIKA ARE CAPTURED

"The missing reindeer!" Rika calls.
"But why are they locked in their stalls?"

Two snowmen sentries block the way.
"No trespassers allowed!" they say.

As soon as Dancer sees the men
He flies into the sky again . . .

"This way!" declares a snowman guard
And leads the way across the yard.

Rika hurries to join Rupert, then gasps in dismay as she peers down at the terrace . . . "The missing reindeer!" she cries. "I can see Dasher and Prancer and Vixen, but why are they all locked in their stalls?" "I don't know," whispers Rupert. "Those guards don't look like Santa's soldiers. They're more like King Frost's ice guards with spiky helmets and icicle spears.." "Quite right!" says a voice behind him. "We're snow sentries, here to stop snoopers and trespassers – like you!"

The snow sentries march Rika and Rupert towards the main tower, then stop to round up Dancer. "We'll put him with the others!" says the first guard. "Right!" nods the other, but the reindeer proves harder to catch than they'd thought. With a single bound, it leaps into the air and flies off into the clouds. "Silly creature!" calls Rupert's guard. "Never mind!" says the other snowman. "These two won't get away so easily. We'll take them inside and show the boss what we've found . . ."

RUPERT MEETS BILLY BLIZZARD

*"Thank goodness!" Rupert thinks "When we
Meet Santa, he'll soon set us free!"*

*The chums see Santa isn't there –
It's Billy Blizzard in his chair!*

*"Hello!" grins Billy. "As you see –
This castle now belongs to me . . ."*

*"I'll show you round – you'll soon see how
Christmas is like big business now!"*

Following the snowmen inside the castle, Rupert
is dismayed at how different they seem from Santa's
old guards. "They probably don't realise I've been
here before!" he thinks. "As soon as Santa sees me,
he's bound to set us free . . ." The first snowman
stops outside Santa's study and raps on the door
with his spear. "Come in!" calls a voice. As Rupert
and Rika are jostled into the room they are
astonished to see a familiar-looking figure. "Billy
Blizzard!" cries Rupert. "What are you doing here?"

"Rupert Bear!" sneers Billy. "More meddling I
suppose! You won't stop me this time. I've taken
over Santa's castle and I've taken over Christmas!"
"So *that* explains the bills!" blinks Rupert.
"Exactly!" nods Billy. "People won't get presents
for nothing any longer! If they want gifts by sleigh
they'll all have to pay . . . And I'll make a fortune!"
"That's terrible!" gasps Rika. "What about Santa
and his helpers?" "They're working for me now!"
smiles Billy. "Come and see . . ."

RUPERT LEARNS BILLY'S PLAN

"This way!" says Billy. "Keep in line.
Now Santa's castle is all mine!"

"More orders!" Billy laughs. "Each one
Means I'll get richer still – what fun!"

"All Santa's helpers know they need
To work for me now, at top speed!"

"But where is Santa?" Rupert asks.
"You've taken over all his tasks . . ."

"All this is mine!" gloats Billy Blizzard. "I'm in charge of everything . . ." He leads Rupert and Rika across a bridge to a big tower, where Santa Claus keeps all his toys. Sitting at a desk is Santa's clerk, with sacks of Christmas lists and a big ledger. "More orders, I see!" laughs Billy. "Be sure to check they've all paid before you send out any toys . . ." "Most irregular!" mutters the Clerk but obeys Billy's commands with a stern snow sentry standing guard . . .

Leaving the Clerk with his ledger, Billy marches into the main toy store, where Santa's helpers are busily at work, taking parcels from the shelves and loading sacks for Christmas deliveries. "Just like normal!" beams Billy. "Glad to see we're keeping to schedule. If Santa can manage it, so can I!" "Where *is* Santa?" asks Rupert. "He'd never agree to charge for presents!" "No!" laughs Billy. "That's why I've had to take control. You can see him, if you really want to. Follow me . . ."

RUPERT AND RIKA JOIN SANTA

"This way!" says Billy. "You'll soon see
Where Santa's got to – follow me!"

"I've locked up Santa, in a cell!
Now you can join him there as well . . ."

A snow guard shoves the pals – "And you
Can stay here, locked up safely too . . ."

The pals join Santa Claus and then
The heavy door is locked again!

Rupert and Rika follow Billy Blizzard down a winding flight of stairs. "I've never been in this part of the castle before," says Rupert. "Neither have I!" shivers Rika. "It's rather dark and cold." "A lumber room!" laughs Billy. "Just the place for things you don't need any more!" Taking a key from the bunch on his belt, he unlocks a heavy door and pushes it open. "Santa!" gasps Rika. "But he's locked in, like a prisoner!" "Exactly!" sneers Billy. "And *you* can join him . . ."

As Billy speaks, a snow soldier pushes Rupert and Rika forward. "What's this?" blinks Santa. "Rika! And Rupert Bear, from Nutwood. Whatever are you both doing here?" "They've come to pay a visit!" jeers Billy. "A *long* visit, I think! Perhaps they'll stay for the whole of Christmas!" Laughing nastily, he slams the door shut and turns the key. "Wait!" calls Santa. "Let Rupert and Rika go!" "Only after Christmas," Billy replies. "Until then, they can stay here and keep you company . . ."

*"That scoundrel Blizzard seems to plan
To ruin Christmas if he can!"*

*"There's only one way out that we
Could try – but it's too small for me!"*

*The window's high, but even so –
It's still the only way to go . . .*

*It seems Rupert must stay as well
But then he asks for Rika's bell.*

"Poor Santa!" says Rika. "Fancy being locked up in your own castle!" "What happened?" asked Rupert. "How did Billy manage to take over?" "The scoundrel played a trick on me!" says Santa. "He arrived in a blizzard, asking for shelter. Then he stole my keys and let in all those dreadful snowmen . . ." "We've got to stop him!" says Rupert. "Christmas won't be the same if everyone has to pay!" "I know!" nods Santa. "I've tried to escape but I'm afraid I'm too big to fit through the window . . ."

Rupert looks outside. He thinks he might just manage to squeeze through the window, but escaping seems impossible – with not a handhold to be seen and a sheer drop to the billowing clouds below . . . "Too dangerous," shrugs Santa. "There's no way down." Rupert thinks hard for a moment, then has a sudden idea. He turns to Rika and asks if she still has her special bell for summoning reindeer. "Yes," she says, reaching into her pocket, "but I can't see how it's going to help us beat Billy Blizzard . . ."

RUPERT ESCAPES ON A REINDEER

The reindeer bell is used to call
The herd when Santa needs them all . . .

It summons Dancer. Down he flies –
"Good boy!" smiles Rupert. "Here!" he cries.

"Well done!" says Rika. "Clamber through!
I've told Dancer to wait for you . . ."

"Up now!" calls Rupert. Off they fly –
above the clouds that fill the sky.

Although Billy Blizzard's snow guards have captured most of Santa's reindeer, Rupert knows that Dancer managed to avoid being caught and flew off into the clouds. He reaches out of the window and rings Rika's bell as loud as he can. Sure enough, the last reindeer answers his summons and comes flying back towards the castle. "Good boy!" calls Rupert. He rings the bell once more and leans out to show Dancer where to fly. The reindeer pauses for a moment then swoops down towards the window.

"Bravo!" cheers Santa as he realises what Rupert has in mind. Rika calls to Dancer and tells him to stay as still as he can. The window is a tight fit, but Rupert manages to squeeze through and clambers on to the reindeer's saddle. Holding tightly to the reins, he urges Dancer forward, hoping to escape without being seen by Billy's guards. "Up into the clouds!" he calls. "We'll try to fetch help." The reindeer needs no second bidding and speeds off straightaway . . .

RUPERT VISITS THE WEATHER CLERK

"I need help to stop Billy's crew
And save poor Santa Claus – but who?"

"The Weather Station! Now we'll see!
I'm sure the Clerk will side with me . . ."

The Weather Clerk soon hurries out
To see what Rupert's come about.

"It's Santa! Billy Blizzard schemes
To take his place – for good it seems!"

As soon as they reach the clouds, Rupert lets Dancer slow down and thinks what to do next . . . "There must be *someone* who can stop Billy Blizzard!" he murmurs. "King Frost might help. Perhaps his ice guards could fight all Billy's snowmen?" Suddenly, Rupert has a better idea and urges Dancer forward, towards the distant turrets of the Weather Station. "The Clerk of the Weather is the person I need!" he declares. "Billy Blizzard won't have thought of him . . ."

The Weather Clerk spots Rupert approaching and hurries out to the terrace. "A reindeer!" he blinks. "Rupert Bear! What are you doing here?" Rupert tells the Clerk how he has escaped from Santa's castle. "Billy Blizzard has taken over Christmas!" he explains. "Santa is locked in a cellar guarded by snowman sentries!" "How dreadful!" says the Clerk. "Billy Blizzard is always up to some sort of mischief. I'll do what I can to help – but I don't like the sound of soldiers!"

"We must foil Billy Blizzards's plan!
Please help me stop him, if you can . . ."

"This way!" the Weather Clerk declares
And starts to climb a flight of stairs . . ."

"A heatwave might stop Billy's game!"
The Clerk tells Rupert, then takes aim . . ."

"This heat-reflecting lamp of mine
Will bathe the castle in sunshine!"

Rupert tells the Weather Clerk how Billy Blizzard's snowmen are all armed with icicle spears. "Just like King Frost's men!" he murmurs. "Warriors from the Frozen North . . ." Leading the way to a platform at the top of the Weather Station, he shows Rupert a strange-looking machine. "This might help Santa!" he declares. "It's really for sending heatwaves to the Tropics, but I don't see why I shouldn't send one to the North Pole instead! If Billy Blizzard won't keep to the rules, neither will we . . ."

The Clerk of the Weather hands Rupert a pair of dark glasses and tells him to put them on. "This machine works on concentrated sunshine!" he says. "It gathers light in a reflecting bowl, then magnifies it through a giant lens." As he speaks, the lens cover opens, like a huge camera, and a dazzling beam of light shoots up into the sky. "I've set the sights on Santa's castle!" the Clerk explains. "It won't be long before things get pretty hot up there!"

RUPERT RETURNS TO SANTA'S

"I'll keep my lamp switched on all day
And heat the castle with its ray . . ."

Soon back Rupert and Dancer fly
To Santa's castle in the sky.

"Phew!" Rupert gasps and mops his brow,
*"The air **does** feel much hotter now!"*

"There's Santa's castle! Now we'll see
What we can do to set him free!"

While the machine sends a heatwave into the sky, the Weather Clerk works out how much hotter Santa's castle will be by the time that Rupert flies back. "It will feel just like Nutwood in the middle of June!" he smiles. "I'll keep the beam shining at full strength until dusk, to make sure the whole castle gets nice and warm . . ." Thanking the Clerk for his help, Rupert clambers back on Dancer and urges the reindeer up towards the clouds. "I'd better hurry back to Santa's castle . . ."

As Dancer flies towards the castle, Rupert can feel the sky growing hotter and hotter. "There really is a heat-wave!" he gasps. "I wonder if everyone at the North Pole can feel it too? Uncle Polar won't be very pleased! He likes the frozen wastes and winter frosts." Mopping his brow, Rupert finally spots the castle itself, looking exactly the same as it did before he left. "Perhaps they haven't noticed?" he thinks. "Billy won't be expecting a sudden thaw!"

RUPERT'S PLAN STARTS TO WORK

The reindeer lands quite noiselessly.
"There's no-one here – where can they be?"

Then Rupert hears an angry shout
As Billy and his guards come out!

The ice-spears shrink. Drips start to fall.
"The guards are melting after all!"

"No!" Billy cries. "It isn't fair!
The castle's my new frozen lair . . ."

Down in the castle courtyard, there is no sign of Billy Blizzard's snowmen . . . "Perhaps they've all gone?" thinks Rupert. Telling the reindeer to keep out of sight, he sets off to explore but is suddenly stopped by an angry cry. "Rupert Bear!" snarls Billy. "I thought I'd seen the last of you. Guards! Take this prisoner back to his cell!" Two sentries march menacingly towards Rupert, brandishing their spears. "Oh, no!" he gasps. "The sun lamp can't have worked!"

As the snowmen get nearer, Rupert can see drops of water dripping from their icicle spears. "What's happening?" gasps Billy. "I don't understand! Why has it suddenly got so hot?" The next moment the guards halt their advance and start shrinking away. "No!" wails Billy. "It isn't fair! Snowmen don't melt at the North Pole. Santa's castle should be icy and cold!" Rupert smiles. "Hurrah for the Weather Clerk!" he thinks. "Without his snowmen, Billy will never be able to take over Christmas . . ."

RUPERT SETS SANTA FREE

*The snowguards melt and Santa's men
Control the castle once again!*

*"Give me the keys to Santa's cell
So I can set him free as well!"*

*"We've won! All Billy's men have gone!
It's back to normal from now on!"*

*"Guards!" Santa calls. "Remove this knave –
King Frost will teach him to behave . . ."*

A few moments later, the snow guards have melted away completely. "It's too hot!" gasps Billy. "I can hardly breathe!" A crowd of Santa's helpers comes running into the courtyard. "Well done!" calls one of Santa's guards. "Billy Blizzard, you're under arrest!" "I . . .I suppose I am!" gulps Billy. "I expect you'll lock *me* in the dungeons now!" "That's for Santa to decide!" says Rupert. "Give me the castle keys and I'll set him free . . ." "Very well!" nods Billy. "I surrender!"

Rupert hurries to the cellar to set Rika and Santa free . . . "Christmas is saved!" he cries happily. "Billy has surrendered, the snowguards have melted and I've got the keys to the castle!" "Bravo!" cries Santa. "I might have known you'd think of something, Rupert. That rascal would have ruined Christmas for everyone if it hadn't been for you!" When they return to the courtyard, Billy Blizzard hangs his head in shame. "King Frost can deal with you!" growls Santa. "Guards! Take him away . . ."

RUPERT HELPS SANTA

*"Wretch!" Santa growls. "To think that he
Could charge for gifts that should be free!"*

*The toy store clerk appears just then –
"We'll give the money back again!"*

*With Dancer picked to lead the way
The reindeer all pull Santa's sleigh.*

*"There's Nutwood!" Rupert cries. "They're all
Asleep, expecting Santa's call . . ."*

The castle guards gather round Billy Blizzard and march him off to King Frost's palace. "Good riddance!" cries Santa angrily. "The very idea of charging for presents!" Just then the clerk from the toy store appears with a bag full of cheques and orders. "I thought you might return these with everyone's presents?" he suggests. "Splendid idea!" nods Santa. "The sooner the better. The toys are nearly loaded already, I see. Come along, Rupert. You and Rika can help me deliver them all . . ."

As soon as everything is safely loaded aboard the sleigh, Santa's helpers harness a team of reindeer to tow it through the sky. "Dancer can lead us!" smiles Santa. "If it wasn't for him we'd still be locked in the cellar." Darkness starts to fall as the chums speed on their way. "Christmas Eve!" Rika whispers. "I wonder if all your chums in Nutwood have hung up their stockings yet?" "I don't know," laughs Rupert. "They'd be amazed if they could see us, riding back with Santa!"

RUPERT RETURNS TO NUTWOOD

The two chums wave as Santa's sleigh
Takes off and speeds upon its way . . .

"Well done!" says Mrs. Bear. "Now you
Must stay the night – and next day too!"

Next morning, Rupert wakes to find
The presents Santa's left behind . . .

The two chums are delighted by
Their gifts. "Happy Christmas!" they cry.

Flying low over Nutwood, Santa lands by the edge of the common, near Rupert's house. "Thanks for all your help!" he calls. "Time for me to start my rounds . . ." Rupert's mother is glad to hear that everything has gone well. "You're just in time for supper," she tells the pair. "I do hope Rika can stay with us for Christmas Day . . ." "Yes, please!" smiles the visitor. "I've finished work for the year, and can't think of anywhere nicer to begin my holidays."

The next morning Rupert wakes to find that Santa has returned to Nutwood during the night . . . "A bike!" he gasps. "Hurrah!" Unwrapping the other parcels, he finds a new ball and a chess-set, with a note from Santa thanking him once again. Rika has a special gift too, which she hurries to show Rupert. "New skis!" she laughs delightedly. "Good old Santa!" cries Rupert, "Three cheers for Christmas!"

THE
END

Follow Rupert every day

John Harrold.

in The Express

ANSWERS TO PUZZLES:

(P.64) RUPERT'S CHUMS
Willie; Bill; Pong-Ping; Podgy;
Ottoline; Gregory; Algy; Tigerlily;
Freddy; Edward; Rika

(P.67) WHO AM I? Skylark

(P.68) SPOT THE DIFFERENCE
1) Chair missing; 2) Handle missing from tray; 3) Handle missing from cup; 4) Label missing from jam pot; 5) Spoon missing from jam pot; 6) Black spots missing from curtains; 7) Sun missing from calendar picture; 8) Button missing from Mr. Bear's shirt; 9) Bottle glass missing from small window; 10) Handle missing from butter dish lid.

(P.85) RUPERT'S CROSSWORD
Across:
3. Gold, 5. Frisbee, 6. Podgy, 8. Elf, 11. Bingo, 14. Zabac, 18. Tunnel, 19. Sheriff, 22. Toucan, 24. Apple Trees, 27. Willie Mouse, 30. Mast, 31. Dollar, 33. Release, 34. Weathercock.

Down:
1. Billy Blizzard, 2. Bell, 4. Lapland, 5. Freddy, 7. Yesterday, 9. Prospector, 10. End, 12. Grizzly, 13. Metal Detector, 15. Brown, 16. Christmas, 17. Sun, 20. Festive, 21. Presents, 23. Reindeer, 25. Wish, 26. Hitash, 28. Skylark, 29. Snow, 30. Melt, 31. Dodo, 32. East.

(P.87) SPOT THE DIFFERENCE? 1. Star missing; 2. Strap missing from Rika's saddle; 3. Stripe missing from Rika's dress; 4. Reins missing from Rika's reindeer; 5. Strap missing from Growler's helmet; 6. Stripe missing from Growler's sleeve; 7. Button missing from Growler's jacket; 8. Buckle missing from Growler's belt; 9. Reindeer's antler missing;

(P.89) WHICH STORY?
1) P.21; 2) P.51; 3) P.80; 4) P.95; 5) P.79; 6) P.36; 7) P.18; 8) P.54; 9) P.52; 10) P.97; 11) P.37; 12) P.30; 13) P.78; 14) P.33; 15) P.8; 16) P.27.